Don't Bullshit Me Daddy

Jon Ferguson

Huge Jam

2023

This is a work of fiction. Unless otherwise indicated, all the names, characters, businesses, places, events and incidents in this book are either the product of the author's imagination or used in a fictitious manner. Any resemblance to actual persons, living or dead, or actual events is purely coincidental.

First published 2012
Huge Jam edition © 2023 Jon Ferguson
All rights reserved.

ISBN: 978-1-916604-09-4

1)

When Mommy died I just told Daddy to stop all the bullshit. I was eight and out from under the tail of the Easter Bunny, and when he came out with the she's-in-heaven-and-happy-as-hell crap I told him it wasn't necessary. Of course I see it all now a little differently than I did then, but for whatever reason I had a hunch even back then that Santa Claus, the Easter Bunny, the Tooth Fairy, and God-the-Father all had about the same ontological status, to wit, zilch. People tried to convince me back then – a few are still trying today for that matter – that it's a good idea to believe in things unseen, but I couldn't see why then and I still can't now. Anybody can invent a whole universe that has nothing to do with what we live every day, but what's the point? Dream? Pretend? Pray? I'd rather live.

Before we go any further, I know your eyes jumped a little when you saw the word "ontological" there in that first paragraph. Of course you don't know how old I am yet, so your eyes shouldn't really be jiggling around, but remember that when your mother dies and you're an only child and your dad's working to pay the bills, you've got all kinds of free time on your hands to read books. And, on top of that, if you've got a daddy that changes continents when he changes jobs, it can give you a whole different perspective on stuff that makes words like "ontological" look like they could be on a damn McDonald's menu or something. I mean if you think about it, long words are really a lot like cows: the first time you see them they look all impressive and scary and complicated, but then when you get to know them you realize they're more like dogs or sheep or something.

As for my age (as if you really care at this point), I'll be sixteen next week, which means I'll be spending a few more years listening to some pretty funny people going through some pretty tough moments trying to teach a bunch of mostly couldn't-care-less morons who never asked to be born what some education department has told them is necessary for us adolescents to know. But since Daddy and I live in Europe now my education plans are a little up in the air.

Before I forget, you also need to know that Daddy used to be a flucking (I read a book once that had the "l" in there and I liked it) philosophy teacher at some tiddlywinks state university in California. That was way before I was born, but he still uses words like "ontological" and "epistemology" and "anthropo-morphic" all the time at the dinner table. Usually when he says any words with more than two syllables, spit starts popping out of the corner of his mouth, the right corner from his perspective. But given that he had me when he was almost five decades old, he's no spring chicken today and I guess he has the right to spit a little when he talks. The good thing about Daddy though is that when he says words like "ontological", he only does it around me, so it's not like he's trying to impress people. After Mommy died we had so much time together that he taught me all kinds of long words before my age hit double digits. I guess he was more than anything just trying to get my mind off Mommy being dead and all. Death, in case you didn't know, usually sucks. I mean seeing a dead cat or fox on the road is bad enough, or even a piece of meat hanging down in a butcher shop or some still wet fly guts on a picnic table, but when it's your own mother lying there never to move or breathe again, you practically need another brain upstairs to deal with it. Actually, now that I think about it, Daddy was kind of my second brain for a while.

Back to those over-dressed long words for a minute. Most of them really aren't any harder to understand than short words. But the fact is, short words might not be that easy to understand when you really get down and think about it. I mean take a word like "cat". Everybody thinks a cat is a real simple thing just running around and purring and eating and trying to get petted all the time, but if you start counting how many millions of atoms and cells and electrons make up just one single solitary cat and then when you start thinking about how all that somehow fits together, I mean the blood and heart and brain and liver and claws and everything, it all starts getting pretty complicated. That's why "cat" isn't really any less complicated a word than "ontological" because all "ontological" means is if something is real or not real or pretends to be real or some crap like that. Anyway, you see what I mean unless you're really a dumbfluck and then it doesn't matter anyway because you'll just go through life watching soap operas on TV and eating French fries (I wish somebody would finally teach me if you're supposed to capitalize the "f" in french fries because given that when it's part of a potato it's no longer a nationality or a language, I don't see why it should be capitalized any more. But sometimes it is. Daddy taught me a long time ago that dictionaries and grammar books are no more true than anything else, that they're just a set of rules that some egg-headed hotshots made up a few hundred years ago and that they're just like rules for a dumb game like Monopoly. Of course you need the rules in order to play the game of life and without the rules there probably wouldn't be much of a game, so I guess stuff like spelling and grammar are what you'd call "necessary evils").

But I'm getting ahead of myself… or maybe behind myself… (do we ever know?). I want to tell you about the first time I told Daddy to cut the bullshit. Mommy hadn't been dead for more than a month I think and Daddy took me to Disneyland to celebrate. I don't mean celebrate in a happy way like when people get married and that kind of junk, but celebrate in a way to forget the pain and try to make life flucking liveable again. Mommy died all suddenly of some strange disease that I still couldn't tell you exactly what it was or is. All I know was that her blood was all screwed up and from the time the doctors told her so and the time she died, it couldn't have been more than a couple of months. The French call it a "cancer foudroyant", meaning it struck like lightning. So when she died Daddy and I and everybody rolled around crying like zombies for a couple of weeks, until one day Daddy comes home with an envelope in his hand that has two plane tickets to Anaheim in it. Back then we were living in Northern California. Of course today nobody has real airplane tickets anymore because everything's electronic, but back then the envelope stuck in my mind when Daddy held it up and jiggled it and said, "We're going to see Mickey Mouse!" Daddy could have driven to Disneyland, but we only had a weekend because school was on.

We flew down on a Friday night from Oakland and went straight to the Disneyland Hotel which has the monorail running right through it and when you think that that part was built in some prehistoric year like 1955 or something, it was pretty ahead of its time. I mean the Walt Disney guy who thought it all up. We didn't really have time to go to Disneyland that night, plus I was too tired anyway so we ate in the restaurant and I had a hamburger with a piece of onion sliced thick like a tomato (there was a tomato slice too) and I remember it was the first time I liked an onion and today I can't get enough of either onions or garlic. Something tells me both are good for your digestive tract in that they probably run all the bad microbes out of town… I mean out of town and into the toilet…. Anyway after dinner we went straight to bed so we'd be fresh in the morning for Disneyland. We each had one of those ridiculous double beds big enough for four people. I went right to sleep while Daddy was reading with a light on. What he probably was really doing was waiting for me to be long gone in dreamland so he could pop on some pay-for-porno film that you get in almost every big hotel in flucking America. That's what I like about America: you get the Bible on the bedside table and the porno film on the TV.

So anyway, the next morning we got up early and had pancakes down in the restaurant and Daddy said he wanted to be the first ones in the park. I had never heard of Disneyland referred to as a "park" before, but I knew what he meant. We rode the monorail over at about eight fifteen and we got to the ticket place before the gates had even opened. We weren't the first through the turnstiles, but almost. What the hell difference did it make? We had the whole place to ourselves – we and the other "ourselves" who had had the same idea about getting there early (at the time, just to show you how dumb I was, I thought the other early-bird kids' mothers had died too…) – and for about an hour we must have gone on ten rides and never waited a second in line. We'd just run up the ramp where normally you had to wait for half an hour and off we'd go on some ride. I wasn't the type to be afraid because I had Daddy with me and I knew he wouldn't take me on rides that would make me throw up or pass out or anything. So anyway… we had just gone on the Matterhorn for the second time in like five minutes and Daddy had been sitting behind me and holding me tight and I felt like at least I had some reason to live meaning that by then I had forgotten about Mommy for a few consecutive minutes, and we were both kind of dizzy so we sat down on a bench next to the It's a Small World ride which wasn't necessarily a good idea because it had been Mommy's favorite thing about Disneyland when we went there when I was six. On the bench Daddy put his arm around me and gave me the line about Mommy being all happy as hell in heaven and for some reason the "Don't bullshit me Daddy" just popped out of my mouth. I don't know where I had learned it or where I had heard it before, but it was up there, somewhere, rolling around in my eight-year-old noggin and out it came right in Daddy's face like the spit he sometimes shoots in mine. And do you know what he did? He laughed his ass off for about ten minutes. Thinking back on it, I guess it was some kind of catharsis or something. But from then on, whenever he says something I know is phony and no truer than Snow White and the Seven Dwarfs, I just say "Don't bullshit me Daddy." Nine times out of ten, he'll laugh again. But never for ten minutes.

2)

There is something to breaking up the everyday routine and doing things like hopping down to Disneyland for the weekend. That trip with Daddy has never left my mind. When you think about all the days of your life that you don't remember one single thing about, it's kind of a sad-ass feeling. I mean it's kind of weird that we do so many things that we remember absolutely nothing about. But I remember everything about that trip to Disneyland with Daddy. I even remember that after Daddy stopped laughing after I told him not to bullshit me, we walked over to a red and white cart that said "Carnation" on it and he bought me an ice cream. Normally Daddy would never buy me an ice cream at ten o'clock in the morning, but he did then. I also remember what kind of ice cream it was. It was called an "Eskimo Pie" and it had vanilla ice cream in the middle and a dark chocolate coating on the outside. And I can still see the girl who sold Daddy the ice cream. She had on a fluffy red and white hat and a cute red and white shirt with short fluffy sleeves and I thought she was really cute and how I wouldn't mind growing up to look like her. I ate the ice cream while we walked over to Adventure Land to do the ride on the Jungle Boat. (Now, for example, who is going to decide if you should capitalize "jungle boat" in that sentence. It could be a "proper" name or it could be an "improper" name depending on how you look at it. Sometimes I think we should throw out all capital letters. At least we should junk the capital "I" every time we want to say some crap about ourselves. The damn ego is big enough as it is... we don't need to WRITE it big. In fact, I've never seen another language where "I" gets capitalized in the middle of a sentence. Even the Germans don't do it and they capitalize nouns all over the place, even words like "chair" and "worm" and shit... and "shit".... Another question is why does everybody capitalize the first letter of every sentence. Isn't the period at the end of a sentence enough to tell you that it's finished? Why do you have to start a new one with a capital? I'll tell you why: because some guy in a big room next to the king's house decided that was how things would be.... And to think kids in school get "penalized" for not capitalizing things like "German" or "Jungle Boat" in some lousy composition. It's the teachers who should get money taken out of their salaries for being such small-minded pedantic peanut heads! But that's a whole other story...)

I exaggerated when I said I remembered "everything" about that trip to Disneyland with Daddy. Of course I don't remember everything. But I remember a lot. Like I remember after we went on the Pirates of the Caribbean ride (I had to look "Caribbean" up in the dictionary to know how to spell it. I don't use spell check on my computer because I like to flip through my dictionary and see new words. When I was in like third grade Daddy had the bright idea of giving me this Big Fat Red American Heritage Dictionary. I capitalize the Big Fat and Red because I love my dictionary… so take that you pedantic pinheads and stuff it up your you know where!) I asked Daddy if he really believed there was a heaven. Of course it was a strange question because I had already told him to cut the bullshit when he said Mommy was up in heaven having all kinds of fun and drinking ice tea all day (Mommy liked ice tea), but I asked it anyway. Daddy said he'd be as truthful as he could be. We were sitting on another bench next to the lake where the big old ships with sails go around on tracks that you can't see because the water's all brown. Daddy said the truth was he really had no idea what happens after we die, but that the important thing was to live while we are alive. I'll never forget the "live while we're alive" part. Maybe that's why I don't spend half my life worrying about my hair or the shape of my nose or if my jeans are cool or not or who's going to take me to the Junior Prom (there is no Junior Prom where we live in Europe) or, for that matter, if I'll go to the Sorbonne, Harvard, or Southeast Hayward State after I "graduate" from the mental institution of lower learning that I am currently an inmate of…

… Anyway, Daddy told me there were hundreds of different religions that believed hundreds of different things about what happens after we die. The only one I remember back then was the Hindus who believe in the reincarnation stuff which sounds like a whole lot of fun but probably has as much chance of being real as Neil Armstrong had of finding a pizza parlor on the moon. But I liked the way Daddy didn't bullshit me then and didn't get me to believe in all kinds of crap. Actually most parents who get their kids to believe in a bunch of garbage only do it because they're too dumb themselves not to not believe in all the garbage that their parents taught them who were also too dumb not to not believe in the garbage their parents taught them who… etcetera, etcetera. (See, when I looked up how to spell "etcetera" I saw the word "esurient" which I had never seen in my entire sixteen years of life, which, in case you don't know, means, according to the geniuses at American Heritage, "hungry; greedy; to want food, to be hungry", and that it was some old Roman who started the word when he came up with "esurire" and "esuriens" – I'm supposed to put a line over the "e"s and the "i" in "esurire", but my computer doesn't do that kind of thing – which also shows you that the geniuses aren't so geniusy because there is absolutely no need to say "hungry; greedy" and then go on to say "to want food, to be hungry"… it's the exact same thing and anybody who doesn't know it's the exact same thing is too dumb to have their nose in a dictionary anyway.)

To be honest, the only other crystal-clear memories I have of that trip to Disneyland were seeing a kid crying like crazy because he had lost his mother (he must have been about four) and seeing the people from Disneyland being real nice to him and giving him a drink and saying they'd surely find his mommy real soon and all that. I'm sure they did find Mommy real soon because Disneyland is only so big and Mommy sure as hell wasn't going to leave without finding her kid. I remember feeling sorry for the kid anyway, but then realized all the joy the kid was going to have when Mommy finally did show up. I compared that with my situation and my mommy whose chances of showing up again weren't so hot and I didn't feel sorry for the kid anymore.

The other thing I remember was that night when I went back to bed in my big double bed. Daddy kissed me goodnight and turned off the big light and then he went back to his bed to read for a while. After about ten minutes I'm sure he thought I was asleep, but I wasn't because I was still excited about everything we had done that day, but I pretended to be all knocked out. After a few more minutes Daddy got up to go to the bathroom to pee and brush his teeth and everything and when he came back out of the bathroom he walked over to my bed and gave me another soft smackaroo in the middle of my forehead. I knew then that he loved me because he thought I didn't know he had kissed me.

3)

The thing I can't believe these days is how dumb the world is when it comes to educating its youth. And when I say dumb I mean really DUMB dumb. I mean dumb to the point of making me want to throw up every day when I go to school and sit in class with either a boring teacher or a bunch of kids whose hormones are so excited that they can't sit still or concentrate for two minutes because of all the beautiful gorgeous sexy members of the opposite sex that are seated all around them, sometimes less than a foot or two away. Even if they aren't gorgeous and sexy, you'd think they were because the kids are so distracted by each other all the time.

Now we live in Switzerland – we've been here for four years – and when we came over Daddy had the bright idea of putting me in a regular Swiss school so I could learn French real fast and meet real Swiss kids instead of a bunch of rich foreign kids in some private English-speaking school. What I'm trying to say is that the whole idea of school like we have today was invented about nine million years ago when they had no choice but to put thirty or so kids in some small room out in the country and stick one teacher in front of the kids to "teach". It worked back then because a classroom of thirty kids was better than nothing and because the teachers could – would - whack the bad kids on the ass with a paddle (in front of the class or after school) or they would make the kid pinch his or her fingers together and smash them with a ruler. I know all this because Daddy's told me that even when he was a student they were doing it. All of which meant that the kids had to shut the fluck up all the time or they'd get nailed. Anyway, the idea of putting thirty adolescents together in a small room today and thinking that is an atmosphere propitious to learning the crap we're supposed to learn is absolutely ridiculous. (By the way when I looked up "propitious" to be sure it was the right word I saw "propitiate" which means… go look it up yourself you lazy turd… lol!) Nobody in their right mind would put a couple dozen – or more – fifteen- or sixteen-year-olds in a small room with the girls boobs hanging out all over the place and the boys trying to all be cool like Brad Pitt or some rap singer and expect them to concentrate. At that age it's hard enough to concentrate when you're alone… but when you're surrounded by all these hormonal bonfires and your own damn hormones are trying to split open your skin all day, concentration is pretty much out of the question.

What I'm trying to say is that school was invented when there was basically no modern technology. Computers I mean. You HAD to stick all the kids in the same room because you didn't have the money to pay a teacher for every kid. Today you absolutely DON'T HAVE to put all the kids in the same room because they all have computers at home and they could listen to the same stuff and actually have a chance to listen and concentrate. (If the kid didn't have a computer, you could buy them one. Computers are a whole lot cheaper than teachers.) The other thing is with the computer you could have absolutely the best teacher in the world teach "everybody" instead of having so many boring uninteresting teachers wasting everybody's time. My guess, when I look around the room in school, is that kids in a class concentrate for probably ten minutes maximum in a forty-five minute period. So my idea to revolutionize the whole damn system – and I've been thinking about this for about a year instead of snoring through Biology class with poor old boring Mrs. Herrman – is to finally use technology in the noble service of education. We could do all the core crap (like French, English, History, Math, Science, Geography) in the morning alone on the computer from say 8am to 11am... maybe six twenty-minute lessons with a short break between each lesson to go to the toilet or fridge or whatever. (I think twenty straight minutes of pure concentration is about all you can ask of a kid, or just about anybody for that matter.) So by 11 o'clock all the difficult "academic" stuff is over and all of it would be done in an atmosphere of no – ZERO – distractions. And I've also noticed for years that everybody is always starving around eleven o'clock and can never concentrate during the last period before lunch, so this way they could eat at 11:15 or so. That last period before lunch has always been just a bunch of growling stomachs and blown-out minds that can't take any more pearls of intellectual wisdom…. Then, after digesting and relaxing for an hour or so everybody would go to "school" school (where is it written in the big wild universe that school has to be done at "school"? – like Oscar Wilde said, "education is an admirable thing, but it is good to remember from time to time that nothing worth knowing can be taught"… or something like that) at about 1pm where they would be put in a room with about thirty other kids and six or seven "teachers" (one specializing in each subject). Here the kids could do their homework for an hour and they could ask individual questions to the "teachers" (tutors really) about what they might not understand. (Even somebody like Mrs. Herrman can answer questions and help a kid understand stuff… she just can't keep a class interested.) There would be no discipline problems because there'd be six teachers instead of one and they'd all be walking around helping people. Then, from 2 to say about 4:30, the kids would have two activities of their choosing – either sports or cultural activities like theatre, art, dance, sewing, music etc. – that they would have every day for an hour and ten minutes each. To keep teenage kids caged up all day in a classroom is total insanity – ESPECIALLY in the afternoon! This way they'd have at least two hours and twenty minutes every afternoon doing things they "want" to do that are creative or athletic. Afternoons would be ONLY for this kind of stuff… (Another part of my revolution would be to have the regular school days go from Monday to Thursday and then use Friday for tests, sports games, tournaments, and cultural events like plays, concerts, art shows, etc.… But I'll leave those kinds of details to the pedagogical geniuses of the future.)

All I'm really trying to say is that to STILL be using the same basic model for education that we had a hundred years ago is PURE CONSUMMATE IDIOCY. When will the world get off its bulbous rear end and create a new "school" system that educates better and gets kids more active and more interested in things? Just imagine, with computer technology the absolute best teacher in the world could teach everybody. And every afternoon students would be active for at least two hours instead of caged up in a room bored half to death. Kids need at least two hours of exercise every day to keep from getting all fat and flabby and to get rid of all that flaming hormonal energy. Any idiot knows this… So why don't the schools do it???

Now the great question of "who" decides "who" is "the best teacher" is a whole other bowl of cherries. But it's like all other political problems… right Daddy? I say "right Daddy" because Daddy and I talk about this stuff all the time. He totally agrees with me, but he says people are serious slaves to their traditions and that the "school" system is a serious, serious tradition. Obviously he's right. He thinks changes will start in about ten or fifteen more years. Too late for me, that's for sure. I'll be out of the zoo way before then.

4)

Another thing I thought about today in Mrs. Herrman's Biology class – it's not her fault she's so boring…nobody could be that boring on purpose – is that nothing that exists asked to exist. When you sit back and think about that – which I did for about fifteen minutes while Mrs. Herrman was rambling on about the mating habits of frogs, which actually could be very interesting if somebody else besides Mrs. Herrman was talking about it – it can really change your whole way of looking at things. Actually I started looking closely at Mrs. Herrman and thinking that her chances of ever coming into existence were about one in eighty-nine trillion given the number of sperms that were going after that innocent little egg that was in Mrs. Herrman's mother's uterus. And to think that the chances of Mrs. Herrman's mother ever coming into existence herself were also one in eighty-nine trillion, and on and on back to before toilet paper existed, and you start to realize that everything is rather on the random side. Then when you think that the brain that ended up in baby Mrs. Herrman's head was not one she herself chose, and neither was her nervous system or her sense of humor (Creation forgot to give her one) and all that, then you realize that everything she really is has nothing to do with "her"… if you see what I mean. Same goes for all the other numbskulls sitting around me. Same for me. Same for the whole bag of tomatoes.

Actually I realize that pretty much nobody gives a shit about this idea, but that's kind of too bad because it made me look at Mrs. Herrman in a different way. Of course her lesson was still boring as hell, but I actually had kind of a tender thought for her for a few seconds as I looked at her ugly hair going grey, her boobs giving in to gravity, the wrinkles dripping all down her face, and I had this vision of her when she was a baby lying naked on her back having her diaper changed with her little arms and legs flailing and her parents huddled over her gawking and thinking that she was the cutest thing the universe had ever produced…

…What the hell…you probably don't care about Mrs. Herrman any more than you care about the assistant director of garbage disposal in the city where I live. Speaking of me, in case you're wondering, my name is Laura Jezabelle Winger and I was born and raised in a town of about thirty thousand that's unfittingly called Pleasant Hill and sits peacefully – most of the time – in the suburbs of Oakland. I say Oakland and not San Francisco because Oakland is actually bigger than San Francisco even though it doesn't get nearly the press the "City" does. I say "unfittingly called" because in Pleasant Hill there's not one hill but about twenty of them with houses spread all around them like fleas on a dog. Speaking of fleas on dogs… the other day I was listening to Al Gore talking on TV (talk about boring!) about saving the planet and I thought if the planet could talk it would probably have one wish and that one wish would be to get rid of Al Gore and all the other seven billion human beings and just let everything else – animals, plants, rocks, clouds and stuff – do what it likes to do like growing, chewing on things, sitting around, and copulating. I had this image that the planet earth was a dog and people were the fleas and all the dog wanted was to get rid of all the damn fleas and when people like Gore talk about saving the planet they're really just talking about saving themselves from getting scratched away because the damn dog doesn't want them on its skin anymore…. Anyway, the town where I was raised should be called Pleasant Hills, not Pleasant Hill, but I must admit it was a rather pleasant place to be born and raised. I got to walk in the hills and chase butterflies and roller-skate around the house and sell Kool-Aid in the driveway. Most of the other kids did the same stuff too, except their mothers didn't die. When my mother died I stopped doing most of what I had been doing, for a while anyway. Some things forever.

Mommy gave me the name Laura and Daddy gave me Jezabelle. Winger was Daddy's name of course. Mommy, who was named Sue Spencer, always thought Sue (Susan really, but only Daddy called her Susan when he was pissed off) was not a sensual name that you could say softly under sheets or next to candles because the "S" always came out like a whistle and the whole word was the first part of the word "sewer" which sounded like crap. So – Daddy told me all this not too long ago when we took a trip up through the Black Forest – Mommy wanted me to have a name that could roll out of a mouth all lovey-dovey and she chose "Laura" because all the sounds were soft and sexy. Daddy said he threw in Jezabelle just for fun because nobody in her right mind was named Jezabelle anymore, but he had hoped my mind wouldn't necessarily be "right". That's what he said anyway. But he's joking half the time so I never know what to believe.

I've got to go to the dentist. Daddy makes me go once a year even though I never have any cavities. When he said when I was about ten that if I ate too much cotton candy all my teeth would fall out and I said "Don't bullshit me Daddy", he laughed and said, "All right Laura, just brush your damn teeth." But he still makes me get check-ups. (Why do they call them "check-ups"? They're not checking "up", they're checking "around", around inside the mouth. The only real "check-ups" are when you go for colon cancer or prostate cancer and they really do stick a finger or a tube "up" there. But if they make you bend over, it's not going "up" anywhere; it's going across.)

I keep telling Daddy to set up my dentist appointments during school time, especially Biology class time (actually maybe I won't anymore now that I've had my revelation about Mrs. Herrman not being guilty of being who she is… just kidding of course), but he insists on putting them at five o'clock in the afternoon.

So I'm off to see my main man, Dr. Nicolet. He's got these soft hands and cute blue eyes that try not to look down at my chest all the time. I don't think I know a man over thirty who doesn't love sixteen-year-old boobs. It's kind of sad when you think about it. Anyway, what I really like about Dr. Nicolet is that he doesn't have bad breath like the dentist I had back in Pleasant Hill. I can still remember not having the courage to tell him so and always trying never to breathe through my nose when he got close, which is hard to do when your mouth's open and there's a suction tube and a mirror in there and he's pulling your lips and poking around with sharp metal objects....

5)

I don't think I've told you about my birds. The reason I want to tell you about my birds is that to me they kind of symbolize what happens – or what might happen – when you grow up. I'm not saying I'm grown up at age sixteen (last week was my birthday) or anything, but if I compare the birds I have now with the guinea pig I had when I was six, you'll see what I mean. Unless you're a lame brain, of course. (To show you what a lame brain I am, I first wrote lamebrain in one word thinking it would look better that way, but then thought I'd better look it up in the Big Fat Red American Heritage – that came with me all the way from Pleasant Hill and hasn't left my desk since – to make sure that was the right spelling. I saw that there was only lame, lamé, then lame duck, so I knew it was two words and I'm such a pussy, I wrote it in two instead of one.)

Daddy gave me the birds for my birthday. That is, he asked me if I'd rather have birds or "bijoux" (that's jewelry in French and I've got enough necklaces, bracelets, earrings and crap already to last me a lifetime) and I said birds, so we went together to the Schilliger Garden Center in Gland where somebody had told Daddy they sold birds and cages and everything. Evidently pet stores are slowly going out of business and the closest place to Lausanne that sold live birds was a plant shop that advertises like crazy about the fact that they're open on Sundays, which is rare around here. Anyway, Daddy and I drove down on my birthday. The place is huge and when we finally found the birds and I saw how much just a little cage costs, I told Daddy I wanted two little brown and white sparrow-like birds that didn't really look like the kind people have in their house but more like birds that hang around your feet when you eat a sandwich on a bench down by the lake. I just said I wanted them because I figured they wouldn't cost too much. I didn't want Daddy spending a lot of money on birds that I might not care about two days later... but you never know. Besides, just because a bird's got a bunch of bright-colored feathers doesn't make it any better than one that's just brown and white. Same thing goes for painting pictures. Last summer Daddy took me to a bunch of art galleries in Paris and in this one there were these big pictures on the wall by a guy named Soulage. They were all black except for parts of the canvas that were left white. Daddy said his stuff sold for hundreds of thousands of euros. Anyway, even the little brown and white birds ended up having some sexy name – the guy called them Japanese Water Ooozels or some crap like that – and even they ended up costing over thirty francs each and they were the cheapest they had. So with the birds and the cage Daddy had already spent over a hundred and fifty francs for my damn birthday and yet the guy kept trying to sell him "accessories" like a mirror for the cage, some junk they could sharpen their beaks on, and this special high-performance birdseed, all of which the birds couldn't probably care less about. I tried to tell Daddy we didn't need any of it, but in the end he bought it all. Whatever. It turns out the cage came in a box and had to be assembled back home, so the sales guy put each bird in a separate tiny little cardboard box about the size of a shoebox for baby shoes. Of course there were a couple slits down the sides for air, but after a nice big cage full of other birds, a little box looked like a rather Godforsaken place to be. Anyway, to make a short story longer, all the way home in the car, I kept thinking that if I were a bird and I had been happily fluttering around having all kinds of fun with family and friends in a nice big cage, and then suddenly some greasy hand reaches in through the door and grabs me and sticks me in a dark little box and then closes the lid and starts carrying me around to God knows where, I'd probably go crazy. All the way home I kept thinking all this anthropomorphic garbage about the "mental" state of my two birds. Were they scared shitless in there? Were they shivering because they were petrified? Were they so petrified that they were getting short of breath and might pass out and even die before we got home? Would they have permanent mental damage from being isolated in that dark little box for more than an hour? (It took Daddy and me forty-five minutes to assemble the damn cage so the birds had to stay in the boxes until we were done. We figured it'd be too risky to let them fly around an apartment they didn't know because they might crash into a window or something.) Were they hungry or thirsty? When had they last eaten or drinken? How long could they go between meals? Would they worry about where they were being taken? Would they feel like prisoners of war being carted off to who knows where? … Then I started to doubt my own dumb self. Did it even bother the birds to be in the little dark boxes? Maybe they couldn't have cared less. Maybe being in a little box was fun for them, like when kids play hide-and-seek and hide in dark corners and feel all warm and happy and crap. Maybe they were happy to have a little peace and quiet, alone, away from the rabble of the other birds in the big cage at the Garden Center. How do birds see the world? Do they have a totally different way of experiencing life than humans do? Are they stoic? Is their threshold of pain and loneliness completely different from ours? Can a bird die of a broken heart?

In case you haven't figured it out, what I'm trying to say is that when I was six years old and had a guinea pig, I didn't ask any of these kinds of questions. The guinea pig was just a damn guinea pig and I petted it and fed it and cleaned its cage, but I sure as hell didn't worry about a zillion ramifications of its mental condition. I'm trying to say that with age – in my case from six to sixteen – the world has become a whole lot more complicated. I can't imagine what it will be like when I'm thirty-six or forty-six or sixty-six like Daddy almost is. I can't imagine that I won't be completely insane by then. But actually when

I look around at people, I lot of them don't seem to see things like me; I mean, as they get older they don't see all the complexity stuff. (I think that's the first time in my life I've ever used a semi-colon. I guess semi-colons are to commas and periods what French kissing is to lip kissing and giving a b--- ---.) A lot of people actually seem to make things simpler as they get older. Hell, for all I know, maybe that's the secret to life… simplify everything and be a dumb shit all your life. I remember when Daddy and I were driving through the Black Forest in Germany and Daddy started telling me about the life and ideas of this guy named Friedrich Nietzsche. (What a cool name! I just looked it up to see how to spell it.) He was a philosopher who went crazy and didn't talk to anybody for the last ten years of his life. Daddy said that for him Nietzsche might have been the smartest guy who had ever lived and where did it get him? … Staring at the ceiling for ten years. Daddy said he spent most of those ten years in bed. He said they think he might have had syphilis and that that's what caused him to go crazy, but that nobody really knows…. Anyway, you get the point.

So now I've had the birds for a week and the truth is my questions haven't gotten fewer, they've multiplied. Are they bored? Do they know what boredom is? How far do their memories go back? Do they remember their mothers? Do they want a variety of food and drink or are they happy with water and the same old high-powered birdseed every day? Do they recognize me and Daddy?

Do they want a cover over their cage at night? How long do they sleep? When do they want to sleep? Do they want a nest to sleep in or are they happy sleeping standing on a bar? When they are on different bars (there are three in the cage) does it mean they're mad at each other or playing hard to get? When they're snuggled next to each other are they cold or in love or both? Are they whispering to each other and calculating an escape, like… Okay Snickers, next time the little bitch sticks her hand in, I'll peck it nice and hard with my freshly sharpened beak and when she yanks it out you slip out first, then I'll try to hightail it while she's grabbing her bleeding hand… Yeah, Caramel, then we can hide out in the living room until somebody opens the door to the balcony and we'll fly out and be free as… as… birds…? I could go on forever. But I won't. But I will say the thing that really gets me is that I'll never know the answers to any of these questions because the birds can't talk. Or if they can, I'm too dumb to understand a word they're saying.

6)

I think I told you that way before I was born Daddy used to teach philosophy at some Podunk university in the Bay Area. Actually it was Cal State Hayward, a school nobody talks about because they never have a good football team like Stanford or Cal or even flucking San Jose State. This was his job after he graduated from college and I guess because he was young he couldn't get a job at a place like Harvard or Michigan even though if I remember correctly he went to Yale and then he went to the University of Chicago to do his doctoral stuff. I'll never forget the title of his thesis which he has kept all these years and showed me not too long ago: "Symbolic Reality: A Socio-Anthropological Essay on the Nature of Reality". Now if that's not a title to stand up and take notice of! He told me he only studied philosophy because his parents had brought him up in a strict Methodist Protestant Christian family and so he had to spend about ten years of his life washing off the paint. I mean when you're praying and talking to God and going to church all the time as a kid, it's hard to get it all out of your head when you finally decide that all those years you were really praying to nothing, talking to nobody, and going to a church that only worshipped itself. If you think about it, the whole process is kind of like brainwashing and whitewashing.

First you get brainwashed, then you've got to whitewash it all away and try to start all over again believing in new shit. I know tons of people who spend their whole lives fighting with the ideas that filled their heads as kids. I mean it's really kind of sad when you think about it. You get born a Christian and it's all stories of Jesus. You get born a Muslim and it's all stories of Mohammed. You get born a Jew and it's all stories of the Old Testament. You get born a flucking Communist and it's all Marx and Lenin and sharing all life's goodies. It's kind of like being born in New York and just because of that you spend your whole life being a die-hard Yankee fan. If your dumb ass had been born in San Francisco you'd have been a die-hard Giant fan. Anyway, Daddy told me it took him about ten years of thinking to finally get all the Jesus and Jehovah stuff off the gearshift pedal of his brain and that that's why he had studied philosophy. (I wrote philopophy first which really looks like a pretty good word if somebody gave it a chance. It could mean something like "thinking done on a couch" or "thinking done by fathers". Whatever.) I guess I'm kind of lucky because Mommy and Daddy never filled my head with marshmallows like that so I have spent exactly zero minutes of my precious little life trying to decide if Jesus or Mohammed or Big Daddy Buddha are the real deal. Actually, some people would say that the reason I'm crazy is because I was never given "proper religious instruction" (to steal a line from Daddy's favorite movie, "Little Big Man", that Faye Dunaway says as she is giving

Dustin Hoffman the bath of his life... I've watched it about eight times) and they actually might be right except that I might not be the one who is crazy in the equation...

Anyway, I'm just trying to tell you a little about Daddy so that I'm not the only one getting all the press in this newspaper. There's nothing worse than some jerk who talks about himself or herself all the time. However, I've often noticed that some people who ask other people a lot of questions so that they don't look egotistical and all are really just asking the questions so that eventually the other guy will start asking THEM a bunch of questions so they can talk about THEMSELVES... and talk about THEMSELVES with a clean conscience because they asked all the questions to start with. What I'm trying to say is that just because some people don't talk about themselves all the time doesn't mean they are any less egotistical than the next guy. It can mean they're just better at hiding it. If you really get down and think about it, is it even possible to exist without being an egotistical bastard? How can a creature exist without not taking care of itself? I mean, I'll bet even people like Mother Theresa, who spend all their time helping poor people, are doing it because if they DON'T do it they'll feel guilty as hell, so they DO do it so they WON'T feel guilty which means they really are just taking care of their own egos like everybody else. Of course everybody with a ten-year-old brain with enough gas in it has thought about this, but I still hear people talking about "selfless" actions all the time and I can't help thinking it's all a bunch of horse manure. One time when I took the last three chocolate chip cookies in the box, Daddy called me a selfish turd and he was right. I've just come to realize that maybe we're all selfish turds, it's just that some selfish turds are easier to be around than others.

Anyway, Daddy taught school there at Cal State Hayward for a few years – I don't know exactly how many but I doubt it makes much difference in the great scheme of things – and finally said he got extremely bored with everything and since he wasn't married and didn't have kids or cats or anything, he had been able to save up some decent money, and when he was about thirty-three he quit and traveled around the world for a year. Back then everybody was "doing" Europe (that's the verb he said everybody was using as if it were cooler to "do" Europe than "go to" or "visit" Europe), so being part sheep that he was, he started there too. He said the places he liked best were always the places where he met nice people which tells you a lot about life right there. Anyway, he's told me stories which make the whole Continent look like a reasonably good place to be. He made his way from Scandinavia down to southern Spain (he loved Barcelona and Seville) and then went to northern Africa. He said he especially had fun in Morocco where he learned how to surf in Agadir and met a very nice girl from Holland who taught him the ins and outs of "serious copulation" (Daddy's words daughter didn't forget) and he had considered making her my mommy, but of course if she had been my mommy I wouldn't be who I am and probably wouldn't be writing. He stayed in Morocco for a few months until he realized that while he was out surfing the nice girl from Holland was sharing her serious copulation skills with some of the other surfers who were not out surfing, so he took a plane to Thailand. Thailand to Hong Kong. Hong Kong to Tokyo. Tokyo to Tahiti. Tahiti to Honolulu. Honolulu back to San Francisco. San Francisco to the Stanford Business School. (He said he decided to see what the business types were like and maybe make some money so he could retire early and travel again.) Stanford Business School to Mommy (Mommy was a twenty-three-year-old graduate student in Mathematics). From Mommy to marriage and a bunch of years living in San Diego where Daddy taught at the University of San Diego. (Daddy told me he just couldn't get himself to spend his time trying to make money, so he did the teaching thing again because it offered the most free time and a decent paycheck at the end of every month and the weather in San Diego was a lot like Morocco.) From San Diego to me. (Mommy also taught a few years before they had me, but she was teaching high school.) From me to Pleasant Hill. (Daddy wrote a book on the ethics of business or some such baloney and he ended up teaching at Cal Berkeley – fewer hours and more money.) From Pleasant Hill to Mommy dying. From Mommy dying to Switzerland. (Daddy took the job at the Lausanne School of Business for, like I said, some fresh air for both of us after watching Mommy get planted in the dirt like a pumpkin seed that'll never grow.) From Lausanne to sitting here in my room writing this book…

7)

See, in case you didn't notice, I was trying to talk about Daddy's life in the last chapter and ended up talking about ME...

But so what? We'll leave that succulent (it's one of my favorite adjectives and fortunately it's the same word in French) subject of the flucking ego and talk about my first experience with the ins and outs of.... I mean here I am, a sixteen-year-old beauty queen writing her memoirs, and I haven't talked about sex yet, except for one sentence about Daddy in Agadir!!! Something's not right, right? So before I tell you what happened with me and my three-day ex-boyfriend, I should tell you exactly what I look like so you can imagine what my three-day ex-boyfriend was drooling all over and pinching and kneading like bread dough. I was only kidding about the beauty queen stuff, but after long observation of beauty queens I have decided that many of them are not really so hot themselves if you take off all the make-up and sexy clothes and especially if you give them a few more years to get plump and saggy. I'm really talking about the girls that are considered beauty queens by all the boys in my school. Most of these girls are the ones that developed when they were like eleven and a half years old and looked like Sophia Loren when they were twelve, but I have a sneaking suspicion that by the time they're thirty they're not going to be looking so hot anymore. I mean nothing against them, but it seems like the chicks Mother Nature matures early are the ones that get old early. In my case I rendezvoused with puberty kind of at the last minute – like at about fourteen and a hundred and fifty-two days – and so I figure I'll stay kind of young looking until I'm eighty or ninety or something. Anyway, when it finally did explode inside me, it left me looking decent. I mean my hips are kind of narrow, I don't have lots of hair on my arms or a moustache or anything (but really, where did this ridiculous prejudice against hair on the arms and on the upper lip come from?...cats and dogs and guinea pigs have hair all over their whole damn bodies and we think that's all cute and everything, but if a girl gets a little on her arms, legs, or face it's like she's got the plague or something!!!). Daddy says my shoulders are still kind of little-girl shoulders and my neck is a pretty good neck as far as I'm concerned. I mean it works and holds up my head: eyes caramel brown (that partly explains the name of one of my birds – the other, "Snickers", is so named because when we went to get the birds at the Schilliger Garden Center we were both hungry on the way home and the only thing we had to eat in the car was a Snickers candy bar which we split and when I broke it in half there was this string of caramel about the color of my eyes that fell on my finger and so I suggested "Caramel" and Daddy suggested "Snickers" and the birds were christened), normal nose a little on the small but wide-at-the-bottom side, lips (my favorite part of me) like they got just the right amount of air pumped into them, face a little wide on top but narrow at the bottom with a chin that Daddy says is still a baby's, hair that is pretty much the same color as the eyes but all that depends on the light too. Of course I've looked at myself in the damn mirror for nine thousand hours! But you know what, I hardly do anymore. From age twelve to fourteen I spent half my waking life in front of the mirror and even when I was asleep I'd dream about what I looked like, but suddenly that pretty much all stopped. I figured my face wasn't going anywhere, I'd seen it enough, and nobody out there really gives a shit anyway about what I look like. I mean maybe some guy like my three-day ex-boyfriend pretends that I'm all cute and everything, but in the end I'm just another trout in the fish farm.... I'm about one hundred and sixty-nine centimeters tall which makes me neither a midget nor Grace Jones, not too long for airplane seats and not too short to reach the cornflakes on the second shelf. I weigh in at about fifty-five kilos which probably would make me a flyweight in a boxing ring.

Before I get to my own actual physical donations to SHAM – the Society of Horny Adolescent Males – I do want to say one last thing about all the so-called beautiful women in our "civilization" (a word Daddy has taught me to use over the years with a forked tongue) and that is that when I see all my friends trying to look like so-and-so, I try to tell them that if you really think about it, so-and-so doesn't even look like so-and-so. Of course you don't get what I mean, so I'll try to explain… If you really really deep down inside think about it, Marilyn Monroe probably doesn't even look like Marilyn Monroe. I mean when you see Marilyn Monroe in some movie like "Some like It Hot" with all the make-up on and the soft camera lighting and the sequined dresses and all, she looks so damn beautiful it's ridiculous and everybody in the audience starts thinking "holy shit…how did God make such a creature!", but I'm pretty sure that if anybody saw the real Marilyn Monroe up close with no make-up on and some fat on her ass and a few varicose veins on the back of her legs and a few wrinkles on her face and some Tootsie rolls around her belly and bags under her eyes and whatnot, she sure wouldn't look like the goddess in the damn movie. I mean we idiots in the audience are too dumb to realize that what we're seeing is not the real person at all and we compare ourselves or our girlfriends or whatever to the person on the screen and start feeling all inferior and shit. But what we're doing is comparing reality (ourselves) to fantasy (the gorgeous Hollywood fabrication on the screen) which doesn't really make sense at all. If we compared ourselves to the real Marilyn Monroe we wouldn't feel so bad…. Well, anyway, I tried.

So I've got a real live body that likes to play ping-pong with its brain, but when all is said and done it seems to function reasonably well. And now it's time to get to my one serious experience with SHAM and SHAF (Society for Horny Adolescent Females) and how I feel and felt about the ins and outs of serious copulation with my three-day ex-boyfriend. Actually, the whole thing kind of left me wondering what all the fuss is about. But then again, just like the ins and outs of serious conversation can vary greatly from one friend to another, my guess is that the ins and outs of serious copulation can vary greatly from one ex-boyfriend to another.

Marcel Monnet might not have been the best choice of the bulls in the barn, but we had been in the same class for three years and little by little there was something about him. Main thing was that he was funny. He made me think that if Mommy and Daddy had decided to make a brother for me he'd probably have been something like Marcel Monnet. So when we finally opted for the serious ins and outs one day after school it felt right and wrong. Marcel was very nice and gentle and all and had brought a 3-pack which he didn't hesitate about putting on. But the truth is, while we were kissing and we were feeling each other up and we hadn't even started taking our clothes off, I'm pretty sure he shot his first wad off. He didn't say anything, but he suddenly stopped messing with me and kind of lay there on the bed saying things like we shouldn't go too fast and that kind of crap and I figured he was just buying time until he could get it up again. He even asked me if we had anything to drink and I got him a glass of orange juice. So finally after about fifteen more minutes of joking around and talking on my bed, I decided I'd take the initiative a little and started unbuckling his belt and pants. This surely did the trick and in seconds he had his pants off and the first rubber around his flagpole. But even having already shot his wad once, Marcel didn't waste any time getting to the finish line the second time. When I asked him if it was his first time he said yes and I pretty much believed him, but you never know. Anyway, we lay on the bed all naked and talked and kissed for another half an hour until we did it again. This time Marcel held out long enough for me to get a little pleasure out of the whole thing, but nothing to write home about. After Marcel went home around six, I straightened things up so Daddy wouldn't know what happened. But when he came home with a couple cartons of Thai food for dinner at around seven, we sat there at the table talking about stuff we had done that day and all of the sudden he said my face had a nice rosy tone to it like I'd just come in from skiing or something, and then he gave me a wink just to let me know that he knew that one of these days – if not that day – his daughter was going to go through the meat grinder and he hoped it would be a pleasant experience.

The next day after school Marcel came over again, but this time we only had a half an hour because he had to get home because he had been late the day before. I knew then that I didn't love Marcel even though he's a nice guy who makes me laugh. The reason I knew was that I just didn't feel like eating him all up. I figure that love is like eating a pork chop: if the pork chop is really

really good you'll eat all the little corners and gnaw and nibble until there is absolutely only the bone left. I just didn't feel like gnawing and nibbling with Marcel. Two days later I gave it one more chance but got the same result. I knew you can't force yourself to love somebody – not in the pork chop way anyway – so I told Marcel we could still be friends and all, but that this would be our last session of the ins and outs of serious copulation. He was cool. Hey, for all I know, he felt the same way about me, but I kind of doubt it because as I was telling him the "let's just be friends stuff" he had a hard-on. But like Daddy says, you never know with men.

8)

Speaking of Daddy, I've never told you why he never remarried again after Mommy died. I sort of know because we've talked about it some, especially in the last couple of years.

I think the nuts and bolts of it all is that he basically decided it's easier to live alone than with another person. Of course he has me, but I'm his kid; he's talking about another adult with the same power status as him. He says that after a certain age human beings develop serious habits and trying to put two dodo birds past age fifty in the same cage doesn't make much sense, especially, he says, "if one of the dodo birds is me". What he means is that he'd rather not piss somebody off by leaving his junk all around and forcing her to smell his shit and vice versa. He says it just doesn't make any sense at this point in time. Plus he doesn't want me pissing somebody off with my junk and another vice versa. He and I are so used to each other – kind of like an old married couple he says – that it doesn't matter with us. Plus I'm his kid and ever since that kiss on the forehead in Disneyland when he thought I was asleep, I know he loves me. Actually on that recent trip through the Black Forest he told me that the only true true love he really believes in is a parent for a child. This is because the parent has witnessed the child's innocence from birth and at no point does one's own child lose that innocence. He says he knows every human being walking the face of the earth is just as innocent as I am, but knowing is not feeling. With me he "feels" my innocence to the bone. What does he mean by innocence? The same stuff I said about poor old boring rotting Mrs. Herrman when I looked at her that day and realized she hadn't asked to be anything she was. Now that I think about it, maybe Daddy influenced me to think all that… but that doesn't matter. I still thought it.

I'm pretty sure he has had a couple of cuties or not so cuties in his life since Mommy died, but I really don't have the details because he probably hid most of the evidence just like I did with Marcel Monnet. I've often wondered why I quickly cleaned up any traces of my official VPD (Vaginal Popping Day) because I know Daddy wouldn't have been mad or anything, nor would he have lectured me on what to do with my life and all that crap, nor would he have asked me hundreds of questions about Marcel and how it all went. That's just not his style. The only answer I can come up with is that I'm sixteen years old and when you're sixteen years old you don't go walking around the house wearing a T-shirt that says "I Just Lost My Virginity Daddy". People do that kind of crap when they're forty or so.

Anyway, back to Daddy. I sort of know that he couldn't live without the opposite sex. By that I mean he couldn't live "live" without the opposite sex. Just because he doesn't want to "live" in the same house – apartment in our case – with a woman doesn't mean he could get by without any female presence in his life. I don't know how many times he's told me how one of the most fascinating things in life for him is the kind of built-into-the-earth reproductive system we have. All species reproduce. If they don't they die out. He says he just looks at himself and since he was like ten years old he could feel this built-in attraction for the curves and crevices of the female body. He says this is why straight men are always wanting to look at pictures of beautiful naked women... it's built into them (most of them anyway) just like a lung or a heart or toenail. He says the only real case studies he's done are on himself, but that everything he sees out there in "nature" points in that direction. Nature for Daddy, as you might have guessed, is everything. When I ask him about being gay or lesbian he says that just like people are born with their own specific body parts, they can of course be born with a desire for the same sex. But most aren't and that's why the species keeps plowing along. Daddy says that it's kind of too bad that lots of religions (Christian mostly) try to get people to feel all guilty about this "in-the-gut" constant desire for the opposite (or same) sex and keep trying to smash it down all the time. (He always says he's speaking for the male side of the equation and that he'll let a female speak for the female side.) Of course he always laughs his ass off when some TV preacher or right wing politician gets caught getting his glory-to-god rocks off with some prostitute or something.... Anyway, he says it's too bad we don't celebrate the Great Desire to Reproduce just like we celebrate Christmas or New Year's or Thanksgiving. He says it's really the one thing that all mankind has in common and that we should have some kind of mammoth "World Fertility Day" holiday every year....

But anyway, now you see why I know Daddy's always got to have something going in his life, even if it's just flirting with a secretary or the cute Sri Lankan woman that has a sandwich shop down by the lake where he goes almost every day for lunch.

One thing I do know a few things about is how Mommy and Daddy's courtship went. Like I said, they were both at Stanford but Daddy had already taught the philosophy crap for a few years and was back to school to get a new degree in Business. Mommy was doing her masters in Math. Daddy told me that at age thirty-three or something he sensed he had had enough fun screwing around with everything he could find to screw around with. He first saw Mommy one day at the campus bowling alley. What's great about the story is that neither one of them really liked to bowl and both were there only because they had come with friends who were bowling freaks. In fact I don't think they ever went bowling again. So Daddy's there bowling with this guy who today is president of Taco Bell or something and Daddy is a little bored of bowling and watching the guy jump up and down and babble the tight-fist-pull-the-arm-down "YES!" every time he gets a stupid strike like he had just discovered the secret for curing cancer or something. So it turns out that Mommy is in the lane next to theirs bowling with a girlfriend and all the balls roll back together on the rack between their two lanes. Anyway, Daddy mistakenly picks up Mommy's ball instead of his own. So Mommy says, "Excuse me, but I think you're holding my ball," and Daddy answers, "Geez, I wish I could say that." (When he first told me this story I said, "Don't bullshit me Daddy," but he swears that exactly what he said.) So Mommy, instead of getting all offended and shit, starts laughing her ass off. Daddy said that her laughing ass was covered by some very nice jeans that had already caught his attention a few times as she had waddled the five little steps to launch her ball. These two things stimulated Daddy to do everything in his power to get her name and/or phone number before they both left the bowling alley. He got both and eventually they got me.

9)

There I go again. I just reread Chapter Eight and what did I do at the end? I brought everything back to ME again. That's what I mean about the ego. It can't be shaken loose from itself. I've kind of made peace with the whole business by admitting once and for all that the whole universe is an egotistical bastard, but that probably doesn't make it any worse of a place to hang out in than if it was a totally unegotistical place. (I just looked up "unegotistical" in the dictionary just to be sure it's a word, but evidently it isn't. If you don't care, I don't care. It surely looks as much like a word as "egotistical" and for me it acts just as much like one, too.) Imagine if the whole universe was made up of purely unegotistical creatures… that is, if nothing cared about itself and just cared about other creatures. If everybody was trying to help everybody else all the time there would probably be worse chaos than there is now. Besides, I don't really like people trying to help me all the time. I like to do things myself and take care of myself. I mean if I lose my purse and don't have any money for the bus and somebody gives me two francs, I'll take it and say thank you for sure. But other than that kind of stuff, I don't really think other people know what's good for me, so why the hell should they be helping me? I look at teachers at school giving out all these punishments all the time to the kids that talk a lot and screw off in class. I think they think they're "helping" the kids by making them do detention and crap after school. But as far as I can tell, they're really not helping them at all, but, more than anything, are just driving home the self-image that the kid is a genuine screw-off who gets attention from the other kids by being an idiot in class and breaking school records for the number of detention hours… Anyway, I had to quit Chapter Eight in a hurry yesterday because I had to go shopping for dinner because there was nothing in the fridge and I'd promised Daddy I'd make dinner. Here in Switzerland the stores all close at around six forty-five, and it was six thirty. Fortunately we live on a nice street under the train station called Boulevard de Grancy and there's a big COOP supermarket right across the street. One thing having no mother has done is make me appreciate all the work it is to cook meals all the time. I think most kids don't appreciate their mothers (sometimes fathers) who put all this food in front of their faces every day. I sure didn't anyway. Until Mommy died that is. Now if I go to somebody's house for lunch or dinner or something and they bring out a big hot steaming meal, I guarantee you I appreciate it.

So I was actually going to go on with Chapter Eight and talk about something that really fascinates me, but when I reread it today I thought it was good to end it with the word "me" for reasons just written about. (By the way, last night I made a Swiss dish called "croute au fromage" with bread, tomatoes, onions, and melted cheese on top. It was delicious.

So the thing that fascinates me is that people always want to know how and where their parents met and everything, but nobody wants to know how and where they were "conceived" – I think that's the word for the great 5-Centimeter Olympic Race where the sperms sprint up the Fallopian tube and one claims the egg as the gold medal that eventually becomes the person in question. Actually maybe it isn't the Fallopian tube. I have to admit that when Mrs. Herrman gave us the lesson on human reproduction she captured my attention even less than during the lesson on frog reproduction. (One of these days I'll google "female sexual organs" and I'll get everything straight.) But seriously, I never hear people wanting to know the circumstances of the serious ins and outs of the copulation that made them. I guess maybe that's because if couples are making love all the time like when they first start out and "can't get enough of those sugar crisps", they never really know which copulation was the exact one that "conceived" the kid. But I have a sneaking suspicion that people usually finally decide to have a kid after their "hot-to-trot" days are over and they're just a little bored with each other and they decide to have the kid to bring a little new spice into their lives. This goes for married people of course. Anyway, if that's the case, I'm sure most of them know exactly when and where they conceived the little critter and that's what I'm interested in. I want to know when and where "I", Laura Jezabelle Winger, first got her start in the world....

So about three years ago I asked Daddy. And I told him not to bullshit me. Here's the facts as spit from Daddy's mouth while we were driving up to Zermatt for a little ski vacation at Christmas and I was exactly thirteen years old:

Daddy, I've been wanting to ask you something for a long time.

What's that? You know you can ask me anything. You just don't know if I'll answer.

What I want to know is, where and when and how did you and Mommy make me?

What?

(Beginning of hairpin turns up the mountain from Visp to Zermatt.)

I mean everybody wants to know how their parents met and all, but I want to know how my parents made me. Where were you? Was it an unforgettable copulation? Was it a forgettable copulation? Was it in a regular bed or in some exotic place like a car or a swimming-pool? Was it multiple orgasms for Mommy? Or even a single orgasm? Or maybe a fake orgasm? And what about you? I'm sure there are differences in various rocket launches...

How old are you?

Thirteen. You know that.

Where do you get your information?

Everywhere. TV. Books. Internet. Magazines. Friends. DVDs.... It's the twenty-first century, Daddy.

I know.

No you don't. You still like the Beatles and your old movies like Casablanca and Little Big Man. If you try to show those movies to my friends they'll fall asleep.

You watched them.

That's because you're my Daddy.

Maybe your friends' daddies watch them too.

Most of my friends' daddies are twenty years younger than you.

Oh yeah. I forgot.

So what happened with Mommy? Come on, I want to know.

(The road flattens out for a short stretch.)

Well Laura, it was a beautiful moonlit night. We were on vacation in Hawaii and were sitting on the beach under a palm tree sipping rum and pineapple...

Don't bullshit me Daddy.

Okay.

So where were you?

In Reno, Nevada. You were born exactly thirteen years and nine months after we got married. Almost to the day. We were celebrating our thirteenth wedding anniversary in Reno.

Why not Las Vegas?

Reno is quainter. I hate Las Vegas, but there's something about Reno that I've always liked. It's like preferring Brad Pitt's little brother to Brad Pitt. Anyway, we used to go up to Reno or Tahoe every couple of years to smell the pine trees, ski, and watch the people throw their money at the gambling tables. We'd throw a few dollars too, but we were never serious about thinking we'd win. Mommy was a mathematician, remember.

Yeah. So what happened?

(Hairpin turns start up again. Daddy looks out the window.)

How many times have we been to Zermatt?

Three. Don't change the subject, Daddy.

Okay. We were having dinner in one of the restaurants in Harrah's, the big casino. After thirteen years of marriage we still had a few things to say to each other. We'd sit in restaurants for hours and talk. Suddenly she said she had changed her mind.

Changed her mind about what?

About bringing a child into the world. She had always felt the world wasn't a very nice place. She had come from a big family and was the youngest kid. She saw all her brothers and sisters having all these kids that were all screwed up and she just didn't want to add to the mess. I went along with it, not because I was of the same opinion, but because I sort of enjoyed the freedom we had and I always thought she might change her mind one day.

And she did?

Yes. We were sitting in that restaurant sipping wine and she takes my hand and says, I want a child. I'm a woman. I feel rumblings in my inner jungle.

She said that?

Something like that.

Now don't bullshit me Daddy.

Only the purest shit gets past my lips…

Gross!

You started the bullshit business…

Okay…and so…

And so I guess her beautiful female body was talking to her…was whispering to her…and she was listening.

Okay, so then what?

Well, the truth be told, after thirteen years of marriage there were still a few sparks left in the fireplace, although there hadn't been any flames for a few months.

Poor Daddy.

Daddy was okay…. So she came around to the other side of the booth – my side – and started kissing me on the neck. Never to be one to refuse a delicate kiss on the neck, I kissed her back. We paid the bill and went upstairs to our room.

(Silence. Wide curves.)

And then? Do you remember any details?

I know we made you that night because the next day she started to get some kind of kidney infection and we didn't make love again for a few weeks. By then she was feeling a little nauseous, so we knew you were probably in the oven. And you were.

Yeah, yeah… but what about the ins and outs of the copulation? Do you remember anything?

No, not really. What I remember is the room… A red

carpet with black dots. Two double beds. Red bedspreads. Framed print on the wall of a cowboy on a horse. TV as always across from the bed on a long ugly desk. Dark brown curtains.

You mean you remember the place, but not what happened between you and Mommy?

It's often like that.
(They enter the big parking lot in Tasche, the village before Zermatt where you have to leave your car and take a train the rest of the way.)

Oh...

I just remember we had a good time. We did it twice. Which one was the jackpot I don't know.

Thanks Daddy.

(They park the car, take their luggage and skis, and catch the little train that will jangle up the mountain to the famous alpine hideaway.)

10)

I kind of forgot to tell you about my birds. But when you think about it, they're not "my" birds at all. I don't own them. If anything they own me. I mean I bet I think about them a thousand times more than they think about me. So who owns whom? If I was still thinking about Marcel Monnet all the time because he had dumped me or something, then I'd say he "owned" me. But he never dropped me and I never think about him except when I see him at school. However, I think about Snickers and Caramel all the time. Since they've been chirping away in the apartment my life just hasn't been the same. I know you think I'm full of nonsense and everything, but that's because you've never really asked yourself what it means to be a bird... to be anything for that matter. (I'm not serious, of course, to say that you've never thought about what it means to be a bird or whatever because I don't even know who you are and for all I know maybe you've thought about that kind of crap a hundred times more than I have. I'm just kind of imagining a bunch of dumb shits around me because when I look at most of the kids at school they really are kind of dumb shits, but of course it's not their fault that their minds have never traveled farther than the nearest McDonald's or MTV show...) And when you really think about it, that's the whole problem: no matter how hard you try you can never know what it feels like to be a bird... in this case, a bird in a cage in an apartment on the Boulevard de Grancy in Lausanne, Switzerland. What I mean is that even if you're all sensitive and care about other people or animals or whatever, the fact is you really don't have any idea what's going on in another head – bird, human or otherwise. I guess what I'm trying to say is that what the birds have done is make me feel lonelier than hell because every time I see them I get reminded of the fact that every brain is kind of an island unto itself and that no matter how hard we try, no two brains can ever fuse. Of course we can do stuff together and pretend we're all close and everything, but when you get right down to it we're all birds in our own cages. I know nobody likes to hear this and everybody keeps sending each other Hallmark Valentine's Day cards and telling each other they love each other, but the more I think about it, the more I think that when somebody says "I love you", what they're really saying is "I love the way you make ME FEEL" which all brings everything back to the world being a great big bunch of MEs kind of trampling around all over each other.

I remember when I was lying on the bed – my bed – with Marcel Monnet after we had done it for the first time and feeling like I was lying next to a total stranger. I mean I had been in class with him every day for a couple of years and had laughed at his jokes and smelled his breath and looked at his boxer shorts because he wears his pants so low and all that, but when the chips were down, I didn't really feel any closer to him than I do to Snickers or Caramel. I'm not saying this is a bad thing, I'm just saying that's the way things happen.

Every evening I put a little blanket over the birdcage so Snickers and Caramel can sleep. Usually at about six-thirty they sit right next to each other on the top bar in the cage which makes me think they've had enough jumping around from bar to bar and chirping and eating high-powered birdseed for the day. It seems like they've got some kind of built-in clock that tells them what time it is. Then every morning when I get up about twelve hours later, the first thing I do is take the blanket away and turn on a light so they can feel like the sun has come up or something. Usually they immediately start making little guttural noises. Then a couple minutes later they start chirping their normal chirps. My guess is that this means that they feel like everything is kind of normal again and that being alive – a little brown and white oiseau in a cage – is not so bad. The other day I tried giving them a little regular bread for breakfast, like I do with the normal birds down at the lake, but they didn't eat it. When they saw it they stopped chirping like something was out of whack in their world. Daddy says maybe they're not strong enough for a bread diet because they've been in a cage and their bodies are accustomed to the high-powered birdseed. Hey, who knows? But I stopped messing with their diets and went with Daddy's logic. They chirp pretty much on a regular basis now.

The other problem I have now is that every time I pull the blanket off the cage in the morning, I fear one of them will be dead. Since I've had the birds I've tried to talk to other people who have had birds and they all tell me stories about how one day they found their bird dead at the bottom of the cage lying in bird poop. Nobody ever tells me they saw their bird actually die. They all say how they came home one day or woke up one morning and found their bird dead. So this has got me thinking that every time I come home from school or lift the blanket off in the morning I might find a dead Snickers or a dead Caramel lying in the sand-like crap the guy at Schilliger Garden Center sold us and told us to put on the cage floor. I know when I talked about Mommy dying in the beginning of the book I made it sound kind of light and funny like it was part of a great big comic book or something, but that was just because I've had to figure out a way to deal with it in order to not go crazy. I guess a little humor has been my way. You know how everybody always says that clowns are probably the most sensitive people in the world and that they only laugh at stuff so they can keep some semblance of sanity…? Well, I guess it's kind of the same for me. I don't want to be melodramatic or anything, but when you stop for two seconds and think of all the horror in the world going on at every second – I mean animals eating each other and slaughterhouses slaughtering cows and chickens and pigs and people harpooning whales and people and animals dying and suffering all over the place for all kinds of different reasons – you've got to come up with a way to not go crazy. I guess most people opt for some kind of religious explanation about some big-time Daddy-O-God taking care of everybody (usually people more than animals) and angels cruising around to make sure nobody gets left out – unless of course they were sinners or bad guys like in the Westerns on TV in which case they will fry in hell and hang out for eternity with the Dirty Devil – and so they don't think about all the horror too much. The other thing I've noticed is how most religions always kind of put animals and plants down at the bottom of the totem pole so that they can slit a sheep's throat, grill a pig, eat a turkey or a cheeseburger, and catch a trout and think nothing of it because Daddy-O-God supposedly made the animals so man could have something to chew on with a clean conscience. The problem is if you don't buy all this crap about god and resurrection and animals being of less value than people, then the whole world becomes kind of a horror show. Of course you've got sunsets and flowers and waterfalls to balance out the gore and guts, but it's kind of a lopsided equation, if you know what I mean. I don't mean to say that life is a royal pain in the ass, but the fact is that no matter how you look at it, you still end up dying and suffering and watching others die and suffer along the way. Of course today the hospitals fill people with painkillers and all that junk, but the fact is none of it is very pretty. I realize me watching Mommy shrink up and disappear during a couple months didn't help my view of things, but the problem is, like Daddy says, I figured out pretty young that it isn't just my mommy that goes, but everybody's mommy…and daddy…and brothers and sisters…and cousins…and aunts and uncles and friends…and cats…and dogs…and goldfish…and…and…and…birds. Like Daddy says, if you don't believe there is a Daddy-O-God taking care of the mess (if there is one, He or She doesn't seem to be doing a very good job), then the only way to survive is to decide to make the best of the days that are left and to try to enjoy the circus while the tent is still up.

So far Snickers and Caramel are still part of the show.

11)

When I just reread Chapter Ten it made me think of something that happened the other day at school. These two kids just started fighting in the middle of class. It was Friday afternoon in English class and the teacher is smart enough to know that after six hours of sitting and listening to a bunch of boring Math, Science, History, French and German, the best way for us to learn English is to watch a film. He does this almost every Friday unless he gives us a test which makes everybody have to shut up. So we were watching "Titanic" and Leonardo DiCaprio and Kate Winslet were getting all hot to trot as she was posing for him naked and somebody else's hand was drawing her (what are the odds that Leonardo was actually making the picture?) while her total-jerk husband was up in the restaurant drinking champagne and hobnobbing with all the millionaires. All of the sudden, behind me, Jerome and Abdul stand up and start swinging at each other at the back of the class. They have time to knock down a couple of desks and chairs and whack each other a few good ones before the teacher gets back there and breaks it up. The teacher – this big strong American ex-patriot – hauls the two outside and yells at them for a while about them acting like morons, then I hear him say, "You've got three seconds to shake hands and make up or I'll take you right now to the principal's office!!!" I guess that worked pretty well because about five seconds later they were back in class and watching Leonardo and Kate get it on in some old car in the basement of the ship. Actually you don't see them get it on, you just see them start kissing before the camera angle changes from inside the car to outside the car. The car's now got steamy windows and you see Kate's hand go up and freeze in the middle of the window and then slowly slide down like she's having some kind of giant orgasm or something. I thought it was ironic how Abdul and Jerome started fighting while the tenderness was going on, but they made it back in time for the real whoopee. Of course a few minutes later the Titanic hits an iceberg and all hell breaks loose and I don't have to tell you the end....

I guess I brought this up because it's an example of people being shitty to each other, but also because Jerome and Abdul both have kind of interesting stories to tell. At least what they've told me is interesting. Jerome's mother and father divorced when he was about the same age as I was when Mommy died. He said they fought like crazy all the time and finally his father threw a wine glass at the wall behind where his wife was sitting at the dinner table. His mother threw her plate of food at the father, then the father got up and left the house and never came back except to get his clothes and things when the mother wasn't around. Jerome's job was to tell his father when the coast was clear. Abdul, the sparring partner, is part Egyptian and part Palestinian and has five brothers and sisters. His parents somehow got out of a Palestinian refugee camp and were finally allowed to settle in Switzerland when he was a little kid. Both of Abdul and Jerome wear their pants so low that their belts are below the curve of their butts. My guess is they're trying to make a statement to the world about a few things they've lived in life. And of course they're trying to be cool. When I told Daddy all this he said when he was sixteen years old it was cool to roll up the bottom of your jeans in real small folds. Then it was cool to roll your jeans under so there were no folds. Then it was cool to have bell-bottom jeans. Then it was cool to wear Gant shirts. Then it was cool to wear silk-screened T-shirts. Then it was cool to wear no clothes....

Anyway, Jerome and Abdul seem to think that the only way to get attention is to create problems. One comes from a broken family and the other comes from a refugee family. Our teachers are pretty understanding in that they seem to realize that they both probably have a decent chance of having not-too-messed-up lives if they can just squeeze them through the system and send them on their merry way when they're about eighteen or so. The thing is that there are so many kids like them today and they just distract each other all day in school. That's why when I get bored I try to think of a new kind of revolutionary school where we wouldn't waste so much time sitting through dumb boring lessons where nobody's listening and everybody's messing with each other and passing messages and flirting and trying to touch anything that's made of skin. Actually the more I think about it, the more I'm convinced that my education revolution makes sense. The Swiss system is all screwy anyway because they have this three-tier system and they stick you into one category after sixth grade and you're pretty much stuck there. Because I came to Switzerland when I was ten and didn't speak any French, they put me in the middle tier. They could tell I wasn't dumb, but I just couldn't talk to anybody. If you're in the top tier you can go on to the university. If you're in the middle one like me you can finish the high school at age eighteen, then go to work (if the school finally thinks you're smart, you do have a chance to do an extra year and go on to college....) If you're at the bottom with all the dummies and knuckleheads you pretty much have to quit school at sixteen and do an apprenticeship. The group I'm in is made of either kids who are kind of slow or smart kids who just screwed around in sixth grade and didn't kiss ass or anything to end up in the top group. Anyway it is an insane system that has kept Switzerland in kind of an intellectual caste system. But so far no politician or anybody has been able to change it. Like Daddy says, traditions melt about as slowly as glaciers.

12)

I don't think I told you about what Daddy showed me when we went on the ski trip up to the Matterhorn. If you've never seen it, the Matterhorn – here they call it the "Cervin" – is one huge upside-down "V" a little bent at the top. When you get to the village it sticks up like a pyramid or a humongous temple. I guess that's why Zermatt is famous. The village is nice with no cars and they have all these horse-drawn carriages waiting for you when you get off the train from Tasche. Daddy and I didn't take one because he always prefers to walk if possible. Maybe he's just being a cheapskate or maybe it's both. Anyway we had a great view of the mountain from our hotel balcony. Evidently there are a bunch of people who die climbing it every year, but they keep letting people go up. Not in winter of course. Daddy says dying doing something you've always wanted to do is a whole lot better than dying doing something you don't want to do, like crashing your car or going to fight in Iraq or Afghanistan or something.

Anyway, we spent three days skiing with perfect weather and looking at all these fabulous white mountains surrounded by the bluest sky you've ever seen in your life, and then on the last day at the dinner table in the hotel restaurant, Daddy suddenly opens his hand palm up and shows me these lumps that are growing in there. He's got two big ones on each hand and then he's got another big lump growing out of the bottom of his baby finger. I asked him why he hadn't told me before. He said he didn't want to worry me and that he had recently met a hand surgeon at some wine tasting event – Daddy loves wine – and that she had told him that the lumps probably aren't dangerous and that you don't have to operate unless you can't close your hand anymore.

I just thought it was ironic that he showed me the mountains – hills really – growing out of his hands while we were surrounded by the biggest most beautiful mountains I had ever seen, just like it was ironic that Jerome and Abdul started fighting while Leonardo and Kate were getting ready to get it on in the back seat of that old car before the Titanic decided to sink. I guess Daddy wanted to show me that there are big mountains and little mountains and both can be dangerous or not dangerous depending on circumstances. Maybe Jerome and Abdul were pissed off because they weren't big hot-shit movie stars like Leonardo DiCaprio and that for them to get the girls they had to do something to get attention… like fight. Who knows? But sometimes I think the whole world is a big pot of soup and everything influences everything else and that trying to really break everything into little pieces to understand it is really just "misunderstanding" it. It reminds me of when Daddy and I were driving through the Black Forest (looking back, the Black Forest stimulated Daddy to tell me a lot of stuff) and he started talking about this guy Nietzsche who wrote a book when he was like twenty-six years old about the old Greek tragedies. Daddy said there were two sides to these plays, the Dionysian and the Apollonian. He said Dionysius was this god who got drunk and danced and fooled around and saw all creation like my soup idea. Apollo, on the other hand, had this idea that with reason and thinking we could figure everything out and make sense of everything. Daddy said that guys like Plato and Aristotle picked up on the Apollo idea and that changed our whole outlook on life all the way up until today. I thought it was kind of funny to think that what people were thinking more than two thousand years ago still influences the way we think today, so of course I told Daddy he must have been bullshitting me. He told me to read a few books and think about it myself and then decide if he was bullshitting me or not. He did explain how religions like Christianity and Islam and Buddhism that were made way back when are still very important to people today, which of course is true, which made me think that maybe he's right about the Apollo-Dionysius stuff.

What's funny about Abdul and Jerome is that if they had other teachers who were more strict and gave out punishments right and left like some people do, they might already have been thrown out of school and be drug addicts in the street or something. Or maybe if the teachers were stricter but didn't throw them out of school, they'd stop screwing around so much. What I'm trying to say is that it's hard to know what the right thing to do is. I do think that deep down inside they understand that their teachers are trying to help them which is probably the only thing that really counts.

One thing though that really pisses me off is that both Abdul and Jerome pick on this kind of fruity guy in class named Maximillian. He doesn't wear cool clothes and is always reading books at the back of the class and never can answer a question when the teacher calls on him. Anyway Abdul and Jerome are always giving him shit because he's sort of a dork. Once the English teacher really went off on Jerome and Abdul for picking on Maximillian and cussed them out for a couple minutes and told them that only weak jerks picked on other kids, especially dorky ones, and that by picking on him all they were really doing was showing everybody how they were all messed up themselves. It seemed to have worked because since then things have got a little better for Maximillian. Maybe the poor kid's name is half the problem…

While we're on the subject of school and growing up and being idiot adolescents, sometimes I wonder if it's harder to be a boy or a girl in our civilization. (Of course I use the word "civilization" lightly, but when you think about it some things are really civilized like airplanes, computers, mobile phones, and good restaurants. Like Daddy says, the question is whether or not these things help make man himself more "civil"… whatever that means.) I really can't decide if I'd rather be a boy or a girl. Of course I'm already a girl and am used to being one and all that, so it's easy to say I'd rather be a girl, but the truth is I'm not sure. Half the time I think it probably doesn't matter because pretty much everybody looks kind of screwed up. I don't necessarily mean screwed up in a real bad way, but kind of victims of the garbage that the media and "civilization" throw at them non-stop. When I look at the girls all wearing the exact same clothes and all praying that their boobs will get bigger and all drooling over the same rappers and film stars, I think "Let me out of here!" Then when I look at the boys with their pants below their butts and their multi-colored boxer shorts waving in people's eyes like flags at the Olympics and I see how they're trying so hard to be cool and crap, I think "Whoa, don't let me go in there!"

Of course there are exceptions, I mean there are kind of normal kids who wear kind of normal clothes and don't say fuck or putain every other word, and who will probably live nice normal lives and have a couple kids and good jobs and chalets in the mountains for weekends, but somehow these boys and girls look like they're kind of made for each other so it doesn't really matter which side of the chromosomes they're on. Although of course the women will have to have the babies and the men will have to go in the army and all that kind of thing. But when I look at the wilder, more hip kids, I wonder if it's better or easier to be a boy or a girl. And I guess the answer is kind of simple: it depends on WHICH boy or girl you are. Some boys turn out fine, some girls turn out fine. Some girls have great lives, some boys have great lives. Some Brad Pitts can say, "Hey, it's been a great ride", some Angelina Jolies can say, "Hey, I wouldn't trade my life with anyone". And some Marilyn Monroes kill themselves and some James Deans crash and burn when they're twenty-four....

So much for that. I'm not going to have a gender reassignment operation or anything. At least not for a while. Plus, Marcel Monnet called me about an hour ago. He said there's this really cute kid in school named Cherif who has the hots for me...

13)

So being the dummy I am, the next day I put a little make-up on – I usually don't wear any except on my toenails – and I put on this kind of blouse that you can leave an extra button open which lets somebody have a peek when you want them to, and I kept an eye out for Cherif when we were between classes. He's not in my class and is a year older than me. His class is about twenty meters down the hall from mine. In Switzerland it's the teachers who change classes, not like in America where the teachers have their own class and the kids move all the time. We have five minutes between lessons, so we can go out the door and see what's going on until the next teacher arrives. Anyway, Cherif is this kind of cafe au lait guy who plays rugby or something, but he doesn't act like he's some hotshot athlete or anything. Actually that's one good thing about Europe. It's not like America where all the jocks are the coolest guys in the school. Here jocks are kind of considered the dumbest guys in the school, because a lot of Europeans think you've got be pretty dumb to chase a football around all the time or spend half your life trying to throw a basketball through a metal ring or skate after a stupid hockey puck and crash into walls all over the place. Cherif has these dreadlocks, but other than looking like he never washes his hair, I think he's cuter than hell. His eyes remind me of the eyes of a dog my grandparents had. They're all chocolatey brown and look so sweet.

I thought it was pretty nice of Marcel to tell me about Cherif because I think he still likes me. But maybe he doesn't or maybe he's smart enough to know that sometimes when you mess around with another guy you end up appreciating the guy before more…or the guy before that or the guy before that. But given that Marcel is the only guy I've ever really been with, he's the only one I can compare anybody to. Anybody like Cherif I mean….

Anyway, the next day at the ten o'clock break I pretended I was going to the toilet over by Cherif's class and I bumped right into him and said, "Excuse me." He said I didn't have to excuse myself and that I could bump into him any time I wanted to. So I knew Marcel was right. We started talking and he asked me what I was doing after school because he didn't have rugby practice and I told him all I had to do was walk home and he asked if he could walk with me. I immediately felt a feeling in my tummy that was very different from the feeling I had had around Marcel. I felt like I was really "hungry", like I could eat Cherif all up in a few bites and I wouldn't even need to put ketchup on him. I knew something was up too because I suddenly got this kind of knot in my throat and when I tried to say "Sure, you can walk with me", it came out all choppy like I was out of breath or something. What was really funny was that it took me a minute or two to realize that Cherif was talking to me in English, something that hardly ever happens here. But I knew he knew I was American and I could tell that he really liked English. It's no big deal, but it was fun to talk to somebody at my school in English besides my English teacher.

So, Cherif and I discreetly met after school at the pyramid in the atrium and sort of ambled together out the door toward the street like leaves blowing in the wind. It's only about a ten-minute walk to my house, but we walked really slowly and made it take about an hour. He kept kind of bumping my arm like he wasn't meaning to and I bumped him back like I wasn't meaning to and I think we both knew we were really meaning to. When we got to my building I knew I shouldn't invite him in on the first day and be all worried about whether or not he was going to try to kiss me or get into my bra or anything. I mean you have to at least play a little hard to get. Actually I think what I realized is that when you really like someone you don't mind prolonging the wait because you actually really enjoy just being with the person. It's when you don't really like someone that you want to jump right into the sex part.... So anyway, I told Cherif I had to fix dinner for my dad and study for about six tests. He told me that he also had to be going which was pretty smart because it was like saying he knew it wouldn't have been a good idea to come up even if I had asked him to. That night – which was three days ago – I had to tell someone and I thought it was too early to tell

Daddy, so I called Marcel and told him Cherif and I had walked home together. I could tell Marcel was trying to sound all happy for me and everything which means that maybe he is a pretty nice guy. Marcel even said he thought Cherif was one of the least dumb kids in school and that the more he talked to him the more he liked him. I said it usually worked the other way around with people and he said that's why he said it.

Yesterday Cherif didn't have rugby practice again and he walked me home and this time we talked all about our families and I told him about my mother being dead and he said he knew (but he let me say it all first) and then he told me about his father coming from Africa and meeting his mother and that they were still sort of together but not really. When we were standing outside my apartment building and his chocolate eyes were melting all over me, I just wanted to invite him upstairs and throw myself in his arms, but something told me I should hold off for at least another day or two. And, just like the first day, he wasn't pushy. After we said goodbye I pretended to be going inside, but I came back out and watched him walk down the sidewalk. I noticed he doesn't wear his pants as low as most kids, which – if anybody's keeping score - was sort of a point in his favor.

14)

Before I go into any more details about Cherif, last weekend Daddy took a little trip to Budapest. What was funny was that he always invites me to go with him when he goes somewhere unless it's for his job or something. So when he asked me if I wanted to go to Budapest with him – I think it was on Monday night – I could tell he didn't really want me to go to Budapest with him, if you know what I mean. As we were finishing dinner he said he had never been to Budapest and had heard what a nice city it was and that he had checked the internet and had found a cheap flight that left Geneva Saturday morning at six and came back Sunday night at ten which would mean we'd have to get up at four on Saturday and we'd be getting home at about eleven thirty on Sunday etc. etc. all of which didn't sound too appetizing to me, so I told him I would take a rain check. I also of course saw a Saturday night alone in the apartment… if you see what I mean. So Daddy went to Budapest alone. And I had the apartment… alone.

I know you're all excited to know what happened between Cherif and me, but first I'll tell you what happened to Daddy. When he got back Sunday night I was already asleep and I didn't see him until Monday night. On Monday night, he told me he had had a great time in Budapest and for some reason I thought maybe he had gone with a woman which would have explained why he didn't want me around. He didn't go into any details about the trip but told me he was going to write a short story about it. I knew he used to write short stories, but that he hadn't written any since Mommy died, as far as I knew. So last night he gave me this story that almost made me cry, because for the first time in my life I think I realized what it means to actually get old. I mean up until now I've always kind of just looked at getting old to be a meaningless fact of life. But Daddy's story made a meaning*ful* fact of life and all I could think of after I read the story was: a) I'd better live before I die, and b) Daddy's going to die too....

Look, I'll just copy and paste the story right here so you can see for yourself what I mean:

*

Walking in Budapest
by William Winger

for Nitin Shanker

Tobie Fischer wanted to see as many great European cities as he could before it was too late, "too late" being unable to walk about freely or dead. He loved to arrive in the heart of a Prague or a Vienna and then just walk. Being originally from Los Angeles, he had immediately been drawn to the tight "old towns" of cities that were built hundreds of years ago where legs, not automobiles, moved people about. Fischer had lived in Europe since college. He had left America on a whim in the early Seventies and had only returned for vacations.

Living in the French-speaking part of Switzerland put him only a four-hour train ride from Paris or Milan. Zurich and Basel were two and a half hours from home. More recently he had started using the cheap flights that airline companies were throwing in his face: Lisbon 49 francs; Prague 54 francs; Budapest 66 francs. The list went on and on and there was always an asterisk saying the fare was one way and subject to certain conditions. It didn't matter; in the last year Fischer had been to Dublin, Berlin, Vienna, Prague, and Rome, each time for the price of a train ticket to Lugano.

He never reserved hotels, never looked at maps or tourist books before leaving, always went for the weekend, didn't care what time of year it was, and the only weather he didn't really want was rain. He always went alone; his girlfriend and twelve-year-old daughter never wanted to come. That was more than fine with Tobie.

Wednesday just before Christmas he found a cheap flight on Swiss from Geneva to Budapest: départ Geneva, samedi 13 decembre, 6h; arrivée Zurich 6h45; départ Zurich 7h25; arrivée Budapest 9h. The return flight was Sunday night at 20h50. One can see a lot in thirty-five hours, especially alone and with no suitcase to lug around.

The airport check-in wasn't even open when Tobie got there a couple of minutes after 4am. He and a few other responsible travelers who had stupidly respected the post-9/11 "be at the airport two hours before departure" rule waited in the empty airport until a Swiss check-in girl showed up at 4h45 with a cup of coffee in her hand and bags under her eyes. She did smile at everybody, then climbed over the spot where you place your luggage for weigh-in, sat down, pressed a few buttons, and within seconds had the airline company operational.

Surprisingly the flight to Zurich was full. Most of the other passengers seemed to know the ropes and didn't show up until after five. When they taxied out to the runway for take-off everybody around Tobie looked asleep and he wondered if he was the only one who had noticed that there were no other flights until 6h30 and yet they sat, engines humming, on the runway for at least ten minutes. Finally the captain came on and announced that there was a leak in the coffee machine in the cabin and that they would be returning to the tarmac to repair it.

They finally took off at 6h45. Tobie and a few others missed the connection to Budapest. At the Transfer Desk they were booked on the next flight at 13h. They never did get coffee on the plane, but in Zurich they were given a twenty-franc voucher which Tobie exchanged for a double expresso, a glass of fresh orange juice, a croissant, and a blueberry muffin.

From Zurich to Budapest he had an aisle seat next to an English doctor from Manchester whose genetic ancestry was given away by hair and eyes, though Tobie had no clue if it might be Japanese, Chinese, or Filipino just like an Asian would have no clue if Tobie was from New Mexico, Toronto, Bristol, or Alice Springs. They talked for an hour and neither even bothered to ask where a grandma or a grandpa came from. The doctor spoke like Prince Charles and they talked about the universal healthcare system and whether or not Tobie's daily intake of three-quarters of a bottle of red wine was too much and if his not having visited a medicine man in fifteen years was risky. The doctor said the healthcare system functioned quite well except for the waiting lines for hefty operations and then gave the standard response that a glass or two with dinner was actually good for you, but that doubling, tripling, or quadrupling the ration probably wasn't. Tobie said it worked for him. The doctor told Tobie to at least check his blood pressure.

The doctor's travelling mate had the window seat. He was an environmentalist whose eyes wandered left and right when he looked at you. He entered the conversation just before the pilot announced their descent into Budapest and had enough time to confirm all of Tobie's prejudices about people wanting to save the planet, to wit, they have finagled man back to his pre-Copernican geographical position at the center of the universe; they never wonder if the earth might not want to be saved (saved from what?); they never ask the question if a clean slate might be the best thing that could happen to the earth; they seem to be like members of high school service clubs or church relief societies who, when all is said and done, are really doing more good to themselves than anybody else in need; they see time very narrowly, that is, the planet might already have been through all this many times before and always came out fine in spite of anything people did or didn't do; they all have a tendency to sound the same, rather like Mormon missionaries; they are strapped to what they are used to and want to preserve a world that might not be as balanced and friendly and moral and nice as they think it is; and finally, they are usually thin and tend not to laugh much. But the doctor's companion, Darren, was a most pleasant gentleman. The conversation flowed, they bantered as the plane dipped below the clouds, and before they knew it, they had landed in Budapest.

On Tobie's suggestion they shared a taxi to the city center. Taking the metro would have been another lost hour in Budapest, though Tobie remembered that the Paris metro had provided some unforgettable olfactory souvenirs. The doctor and Darren (in the taxi he said he worked on "durable projects" which made Tobie think he had probably never read Heraclitus) had reservations at the Intercontinental which, they said, was optimally located right on the Danube. Tobie would ride with them to their hotel, then head out to wherever from there.

The first thing that popped up as their taxi scooted out of the airport was a McDonald's. The driver spoke enough English to tell them that there were twenty-one McDonald's in and around Budapest. He made this sound neither good nor bad. He proceeded to drive like an ambulancier, getting them to their destination in what must have been record time. Normally Tobie would have been "scared shitless" (the precise expression which crossed his mind as they weaved in and out of traffic), but he had recently been to Rome which reduced his trepidation. He wondered if the driver had somehow divined that he had lost one-sixth of his time in Budapest to a faulty coffee machine and was trying to rectify the injustice. In any case, happy to be alive and whole at the entrance to the Intercontinental, Tobie gave the cabbie a healthy tip. It was almost Christmas and they'd all be dead reasonably soon anyway.

Tobie shook hands with Chen (he gave his name at the end) and Darren (to whom Tobie gave his email address just before landing) and warm goodbyes were exchanged. The doctor and the environmentalist slipped into their hotel. Tobie stood on the sidewalk and looked around. It was already nearly four o'clock in the afternoon and dusk seemed to be charging up the Danube past the bridge that loomed to his left. The river was much wider than he had expected.

He started to walk away from the water into the Pest part of town. He would look for a cheap quaint hotel. All he carried was a small, aged shoulder-bag that contained a change of socks and underwear and the necessities for tooth care. The bag was leather and its shape and size had, over the years, incited many people to wonder if Tobie might not be gay. He wasn't, though he had often wished he were bisexual such that his odds of finding love in this world would instantly double. But, alas, at age sixty all he had known were the ups and downs of living and lovemaking with women.

It was at least –5 out. Tobie extracted the hideous turquoise hunting cap that he always kept in the left pocket of his winter coat. It had a long brim and flaps to cover ears. From the right pocket he withdrew his grey woolen gloves. He was prepared. He had put on his long underwear twelve hours before in the dark of his bedroom and had covered it with black jeans, a charcoal turtleneck sweater, and later an alpaca scarf. He had hesitated to wear heavy boots, but decided on thick socks and the comfort of his everyday brown loafers. As he began to meander, he noticed that the locals were as prepared as he was for the weather. Nobody looked cold except an adorable young woman sitting at an outdoor table giving information to tourists. When Tobie passed her she smiled as she rubbed her mittens together and rocked back and forth on a stool. Tobie smiled back, crossed his arms, and said "Brrr".

He strolled in front of another five-star hotel, then turned right into a crowded pedestrian street with signs that announced Armani, Gucci, Adidas, C&A, and other such names that whispered that the Berlin Wall had fallen quite a while ago. There was also another McDonald's that was discreetly housed in a beautiful building that had to have been at least four or five centuries old.

Tobie soon found himself in a huge square filled by a Christmas market. There were lines of little chalet-like booths with strings of lights that shone down on counters and displays of mostly handmade goods. People – as thick as the masses that used to head for the exit turnstiles after a Dodger-Giant game that had been won in the bottom of the tenth inning – were moving about like blood being squeezed through a vein. When Tobie finally got to the other side he found himself standing between a huge Christmas tree and a band that was playing music that didn't seem to have much to do with the holiday season. He decided he would come back the next morning to buy some presents before the afternoon throng arrived.

It was dark. He had walked for thirty minutes and still hadn't seen a hotel. In Paris or Rome there were hotels on every corner. But he wasn't worried; visitors had to sleep somewhere. He took the Apaczal Csere Janos Avenue for two long blocks, then went up a side street. It was time for a beer or a glass of Hungarian white wine. Friends in Switzerland had told him that the local Tokays were very good. He found a little café and ordered a beer. There were few customers and when he inquired about white wine the man behind the bar seemed more than happy to practice his English. He suggested a dry Tokay which Tobie accepted. He asked the man if there were any quaint hotels nearby. The man pointed toward the river and said there were three or four down to the left by the white bridge. Did Tobie know where the white bridge was? Yes, he had seen it coming into town. It wasn't far, maybe ten or twelve minutes.

Tobie didn't find three or four hotels, but one was enough. It was next to a parking lot next to the white bridge and the long metal door handle was broken in the middle. But the man at the reception desk was as pleasant as the man in the café. For fifty-six euros Tobie was escorted to a room with a large bed, a small TV, a desk, chair, toilet, and shower. He thanked the man, took his socks, change of underwear, and tooth supplies out of his bag, and without taking off his scarf, hat, or coat, was back on the streets of Budapest in less than a minute.

He walked briskly along the river back toward the other bridge up by the Intercontinental Hotel, dodged a car and crossed the road to the Szécheny bridge. He looked out toward the Buda side of town and the lights of the castle and the old buildings on top of the hill.

There was a beggar on the bridge. Tobie had only Swiss change and told him he'd sort something on the way back. The river looked like the sky. Both had glitter on the black velvet. People walked quickly.

How long is this bridge? Two... three football fields? More?

On the other side there was a cable car going straight up the hill. Cars buzzed left and right. Tobie could see a small quiet road that angled toward the castle. A woman was standing at the crosswalk under a streetlamp.

"Excuse, me. What is the best way to get up to the castle?"

The woman turned. She was young and from what Tobie could see looked like Amber Heard. She had a hat pulled low on her head and a scarf around her neck and chin. But she had the nose, eyes, and lips – slightly turned down at the corners – of Vanessa Paradis.

"You can take the cable car there, or you can walk."

"Which way?"

"That way, there." She pointed to the road Tobie had seen.

"Thank you. Your English is very good."

"Actually I'm here in Budapest for an English examination. It's kind of like the Toffel test. I had the choice of taking it in Kyiv or Budapest, but Budapest was closer."

"Where do you live?"

"In Ukraine. I'm Ukrainian."

"And it was closer to come here than go to Kyiv?"

"Yes." (Tobie had no idea what the map looked like.) "I took the train yesterday and I had the test this morning."

"How did you do?"

"I think I passed okay."

Tobie rubbed the earmuff part of his turquoise hat and pulled the brim lower. "Well, I guess I'll walk up here. Thanks."

He started to walk. She walked with him.

In the dark with my hat on she probably can't tell how old I am. Maybe she doesn't care.

"So what school do you go to?"

"I finished university a year ago. Now I work for an American company."

"So why did you need to take this test today?"

"I need the certificate to go to school in England. I want to do a Masters there."

"In what?"

"Business management, I guess."

She gestured to the right. They turned off the road, walked through a portal, and started up some steep steps. The steps began to crisscross. Tobie stopped for a few seconds and looked at the Danube and the lights of Pest. She stopped next to him.

"And you? What do you do?"

"I work in Switzerland."

"What kind of work?"

"I buy and sell things some people need."

"What kind of things?"

"Things that keep your heart from stopping."

"You're not Swiss, are you? You don't sound Swiss."

"No, I'm originally from California. Los Angeles. Have you been there?"

"No, it's expensive. But I'd like to go. I'd like to go everywhere."

Everywhere? What a joy to be able to walk. What a joy to be able to talk.

They reached the top of the hill. She pointed. "Over there is where the President is supposed to live, but I don't know if he really lives there." She took a few steps toward a wall. "Come here. Look at this." Her index pointed to some silver dollar-sized holes in the wall. "This is where they shot at the demonstrators in 1956."

Tobie had been in Berkeley in 1968 when policemen on the roofs around Telegraph Avenue were shooting rubber bullets to disperse demonstrators. These bullets hadn't been rubber.

What a world. God bless America. God bless Hungary. God bless China. God bless Mars.

"How do you know Budapest so well? Have you lived here?"

"No, but I've been here five or six times. I'm meeting a girlfriend tomorrow."

"What's this way?"

"It's beautiful. Let's go this way."

They climbed a few more steps and walked to a point that gave them a view of everything.

"It's absolutely beautiful up here. Why aren't there any tourists?"

"It's too cold. They come up in the day."

"Oh."

They walked past a large church with a checkered roof and steeple, then along a street that looked like the one Mozart lived in in the film "Amadeus". Cobblestones. Yellow or white buildings.

"I can't believe there's nobody up here. Pest was packed with people, and here nobody."

"There's a Hilton Hotel over there. I think it's the only one up here, but I'm not sure." Two couples approached on the other side of the street. They went into a restaurant.

"Well, it's amazingly beautiful. Thanks for the tour."

"I was coming here anyway. It's my favorite place. Especially at night." Her boots clanged on the cobblestones. Tobie noticed she had the same way of lifting her knees that his girlfriend in college had. Bonnie Hilton. No relation to the hotel. He had thought her the most gorgeous, sexiest, sleekest creature ever to toe the planet. They had talked about getting married their senior year. Bonnie got pregnant during the summer by another guy.

"You know, you walk just like a girlfriend I used to have in college. Like a catwalker."

"What's a catwalker?"

"Like a model on a runway."

"I thought runways were for airplanes." She laughed.

They made a loop and came back where the Hilton Hotel was. They could see people inside the restaurant.

"Are you hungry? Or thirsty? I'm both actually."

"Not really."

She led him to another viewpoint that looked like it had been a fortress. They stopped.

"That's the Parliament over there." She pointed left. "I like the bridges."

She can't be over twenty-five. She said she'd finished school and now worked for an American company. In Switzerland a lot of

Ukrainian women come to work in the cabarets to make some quick money and then go back home. Some try to find a husband. I don't even know her name. "What's your name? I don't even know."

"Valentina."

"Nice name. My name's Tobie."

"Is that like 'To be or not to be?' I tried to read Shakespeare, but it's hard for foreigners."

"It's hard for non-foreigners."

"Let's go down this way." She pointed to some steps through another portal. Halfway down the steps a young man with beige hair dripping from his cap was playing a violin. Another hat on the ground in front of him didn't have much money in it. How could it? They probably hadn't seen a dozen people in forty-five minutes. Tobie couldn't believe the guy was standing there playing music in –5 weather. The man had gloves on that were cut off in the middle of the fingers. Valentina dropped some coins. The man nodded, adjusted his hat, and started playing Vivaldi.

They kept walking down. As they neared the river Tobie asked Valentina if she knew what time it was. She looked at her telephone. "It's seven fifteen."

Tobie saw a wine bar. "Can I offer you a drink? I'm hungry, but we can get a drink in here at least."

"Okay."

They went into the wine bar. It was very cozy, well-lit, but empty. There were stand-up menus on the tables. The waiter came quickly and ushered them to a table next to the window with a view of the Danube.

"I'd just like a glass of Hungarian red wine," Tobie said. "Would you like some wine, Valentina?"

"No, I'll have some tea. Do you have green tea?"

"Yes," the waiter said. "Any preference for the wine, sir?" His English was excellent.

"Just a good local wine."

"They're all local."

"Then you choose."

Tobie took off his hat. Valentina did the same. They could see each other now, in a sense. He mussed his hair. If he had anything at his age, it was hair. His hairline hadn't moved since college. Actually he still had most of his body. They put their coats on the backs of their chairs. Tobie looked at Valentina's hands. They looked like a young girl's with long fake fingernails.

"How old are you Valentina?"

"What do you think?"

"Twenty-one. Twenty-two."

"Twenty-four." She pushed a handful of brownish-blonde curls off her face. "What about you?"

"Guess."

"Fifty. Fifty-two."

"Thanks. I just turned sixty."

"That's how old my dad is."

"Are your parents still together?"

"Yes. They still live in the same house."

The only guys my age who sleep with beautiful young women are movie stars and presidents. Jack Nicholsons and Bill Clintons. But my father was right when he told me that the problem with being sixty is that your eyes still feel twenty-five. Like I told somebody – who was it? – a few weeks ago: the tragedy of life is not that you die, but that you can't make love to all the people you would like to before you die.

"They're both retired now."

"You sound like you love them and you look like you had a very happy childhood."

"I did. I still am happy. Do I look happy? I just broke up with my boyfriend today."

She just broke up with her boyfriend? She looks like she just got a puppy for Christmas.

"Actually that was one of the other reasons I came to Budapest for the test. I hadn't seen him for three months. We decided it was too hard being so far apart."

"How old was he?"

"Thirty-one."

Well, that's halfway anyway. Am I insane? Of course I am. But remember in that anthropology class there were some African tribes where the old village chief gets to – has to – deflower all the virgins. Some American Indian tribes respected the old men such that they became the desired men. Good luck asshole.

The waiter brought the tea and wine. Tobie swirled the liquid and put his nose inside the glass while Valentina's lovely hands manipulated the teapot.

"It's a pinot noir made not too far from here. Up north a little," the waiter said.

"It'll be fine."

The waiter disappeared.

"Was it difficult? The separation."

"He's a nice guy. I'm sure we'll see each other again. But we're a five-hour train ride from each other, so we both thought it would be better."

One side always thinks it's "better" than the other. These things are never perfectly balanced. So what? Why should they be?

"So do you sell millions of things to keep hearts going."

"Millions."

"What else do you do?"

"I write stories."

"About what?"

"Life. Whatever. You. Me. Anything." He sipped his wine. He looked at the Danube. She looked at the teapot then blew into her cup. "Recently somebody asked me what literature was. I said literature was a way to share a view of the world with friends mostly unknown. I guess that's it. That's why I write the stories. To have somebody to talk to."

"I wrote a book when I was ten. I was talking to myself. It was one of the most fun things I've ever done."

"See, that's it. Everybody makes such a big deal out of writing. But it's not a big deal. It's just a way to try to make contact with whatever is out there." Oh my godless god. I need another glass of wine.

Tobie got the waiter's attention and asked him to bring him a different wine. He wanted to sample Hungary.

"So what's your job, Valentina? What do you do?"

"I'm kind of an accountant, but I do lots of things. That's what I like about it."

Lots of things? Oh heaven help those who cannot help themselves. I wonder what her boss looks like.

"But I really want to go back to school. I think I want to start my own company one day."

"That's great. Why not? It's always better to work for yourself than somebody else." Tobie picked up the stand-up menu. They served food. He had to eat. He'd probably walked six kilometers and hadn't eaten since a little sandwich on the plane. "Wouldn't you like to eat something? I'm starved."

"No, really. I had some soup back at the hotel at about five. But go ahead."

"I'll get a plate of cold cuts and you can nibble if you want something."

"What is 'nibble'? It sounds like 'nipple'. I know nipple from an art class."

I hope I live to remember this night. She is so cute. Down boy. You have more chance of becoming president of Hungary than nibbling her nipple.

"It's kind of like taking bits of food with your fingers and munching on them."

"Oh, okay. I might nibble then."

The waiter. Another glass of wine. The food. The Danube. Valentina. A group of six people came in and sat at the table next to them. They spoke Hungarian. Tobie couldn't understand a single word. Valentina nibbled. Tobie nibbled and drank.

He finally ordered a dessert wine. That Valentina sipped.

When they got up to leave it was after ten o'clock. Both bundled up again. Tobie thanked the waiter profusely. He held the door for Valentina.

They walked to the river.

"Which way is your hotel?" Tobie asked.

"That way."

"Mine's that way." Tobie indicated the other way.

"Let's go look at that big church over there." Over there was Tobie's way, across the bridge.

"Sure," said Tobie.

Tobie and Valentina walked back across the Szécheny bridge.

Whatever happens, I'll have a story to tell.

It was the St. Stephen's Basilica, but Tobie wouldn't know it until the next day. They were the only ones walking toward it. There was a huge Nativity scene in the plaza.

"Do you believe in God?" he asked.

"I believe in something."

People always say they believe in something. What could that something be? A friend? A foe? A guardian angel? A baseball team? A kick in the butt? A kiss on the neck? A nipple? Would that something enjoy chocolate cake or a hand in a crotch?

"My parents are Catholic."

"Do they believe in Catholicism? The Pope?"

"Yes."

"Do you?"

"I don't know. But I believe in something more than just us."

Just us.… For the last four hours there has been just us. I will never forget you Valentina. A sixty-year-old man who feels thirty, like your boyfriend, who looks decent for his age, who lives with a woman to whom, for whatever reason, love is rarely made anymore. How many sixty-year-olds make love on a regular basis? No, I will never forget you Valentina. Walking with you in Budapest. Believe me, I don't have my hopes up. I have learned to expect nothing.

"You know, a force greater than us. What about you?"

"I have no idea. For me all existence is an amazing mystery."

They kept walking, now in the direction of Tobie's hotel. They went through the empty Christmas market.

"This market was absolutely full of people this afternoon. I'm going to come back in the morning to get a couple of presents. For my daughter."

Valentina didn't say anything. When they were less than fifty meters from his hotel, Tobie said, "Valentina, I know you're a long way from your hotel and it's late. It must be almost midnight. If you want to sleep here you're welcome to. I have two beds."

The "two beds" thing was not really a lie because in the minute he had spent in the room that afternoon he had seen two duvets on a large bed. He had thought it was two single beds pushed together like they often do in Switzerland.

Now they were standing in front of the hotel. "And don't worry, I promise you I wouldn't do anything you didn't want to do. I'm not that kind of a man."

She looked at his chest for a few seconds. "I guess I'd better go. I can take the bus back."

"Okay," Tobie said reaching for her hand. "It's been a pleasure."

They exchanged cheek kisses. She turned and catwalked away.

The next morning Tobie checked out of the hotel at nine. He walked to the Christmas market and bought the presents for his daughter. Then he walked all the way down Andrassy to the zoo, the Fine Arts Museum, and the public baths. He had done them all by noon. He had six hours before he needed to leave for the airport. He walked the three kilometers back to the Szécheny bridge. From there he retraced the route he had taken with Valentina the night before stopping only in a restaurant near the Hilton for the only hot meal he would have in Budapest. At four-thirty his legs were very tired. He took the metro and a bus to the airport arriving there three hours before his flight back to Geneva.

She found him on Facebook and sent him a message a week later. They have communicated a few times since. Yesterday morning she asked him if he would be so kind as to correct her letter of motivation for the Masters program in London. He did. He knows that unless he loses his mind he will always remember walking in Budapest. What he doesn't know is which he will remember more clearly, the walk at night with Valentina or the solitary walk under grey skies the following afternoon.

*

So that's the story. My Dad. Budapest. I guess he didn't go with a woman after all. Of course I asked him how much of it was true and he said about 98.99% which was what I figured. Then I asked him who Nitin Shanker was (the guy he dedicated the story to) and he said he was a colleague from India who is always worrying about not being able to seduce young beautiful women anymore. Other than that we didn't really talk about the story or anything else that might have happened in Budapest. I just told him I loved it which I hope he understood to mean that I loved him.

As I read the story I realized I haven't even mentioned what time of the year it is. I guess that's because I hardly notice the weather much because I'm so distracted and fascinated by all the human stuff going on around me. I think people who are bored are the ones who are always worrying about the weather because they've got nothing else to think about. I figure the weather doesn't care about me, so why should I care about it. It gets cold, put on a few layers of clothes; it gets hot, take them off (second semi-colon in my life). Anyway, it's almost Christmas like in Daddy's story. We still kind of celebrate Christmas with a little tree and a couple of presents. Daddy always cooks our only turkey dinner of the year with mashed potatoes, stuffing, cranberry sauce, and Brussel sprouts. The last few years we've usually gone somewhere for a few days…. But you probably don't care about all that. But I'll bet you do care about what's going on with Cherif….

15)

Walking in Lausanne
by Laura Winger

for Enibuddy Hookares

Jenny Fischer had lived in Lausanne for almost six years. She had come with her father who had wanted to get her into a fresh fish tank after her mother was one day found floating on her side and was buried four days later. Jenny had been eight. They made the move when she was ten. Her daddy taught in the Lausanne School of Business. Leaving America had given her a new perspective on life. Two fish tanks. Two perspectives. Her daddy had not come home with a new mommy for Jenny and this suited her just fine. She and her daddy lived happily in a nice big apartment with a view of the lake and mountains on a quaint street called the Boulevard de Grancy.

Jenny was sixteen and in tenth grade in school and swimming in the fish tank was a reasonably smooth affair. She got good grades; she sold her virginity to a friend in exchange for a few good laughs; her body had developed to a point where boys looked at her when she approached though she was not the type to wear clothes that had the males dreaming of taking them off; she thought most kids were pretty dumb, but that didn't mean they weren't fun to be around.

Jenny and her father often took little trips together to places like Alsace or the Burgundy region in France, the Black Forest in Germany, or the four-hour train ride to Paris or Milano. Jenny had seen a lot in the six years that she had lived in Lausanne which was a good thing because it helped keep her mind off Mommy in the soil. So when her father proposed a little weekend trip to Budapest, her immediate thought was "pourquoi pas?" But when he explained that they would be leaving the house at 4am on a Saturday and coming home at 11pm on a Sunday, Jenny decided she'd let her daddy go alone. Plus, she imagined he saw enough of her and that he might even have had a woman in mind if she said no. Of course he could have a woman in mind if she said yes, but that wasn't his style. One mother had been enough for her to have and enough for her to lose.

It so happened that exactly six days before her daddy went to Budapest, Jenny bumped into the first boy who ever really made her inner jungle jingle. His name was Adrian and his class was twenty meters away from her class on the same floor in the same school. Adrian was a shy and reserved type. However, when a friend named Marcello told him that he had done it with Jenny, but now they were just friends, Adrian told Marcello that he thought Jenny was really cool. Marcello, being one to help a friend in need, told Jenny that Adrian thought she was the coolest thing since ice. So the next day at school Jenny made a point of accidentally on purpose bumping into Adrian and Adrian put one and one together and started talking to her and eventually asked her if he could walk home with her after school that day. They had a great walk and talk. Two days later they had another great walk and talk. Two days later her father was on a plane to Budapest and she was home as alone as an eagle on top of a telephone pole in mating season. Daddy left the house at 4am to catch his plane. Adrian was at her door at 9am.

She showed him her room and the view from the balcony and Adrian said the apartment was beautiful. Then they went to the kitchen that opened onto the dining room. She offered him some orange juice and a day-old croissant. He politely refused. She introduced him to her birds.

"Hi birdies," she said. "I say 'Hi birdies' every morning and every time I come home. This is Caramel…this one…here…and that one is Snickers."

"Which one?"

"The one with more brown feathers."

"It's hard to tell which is which."

"I know. My daddy still can't tell them apart."

Snickers and Caramel chirped. Jenny went on in all sincerity. "They have sort of changed my life… I mean my outlook on life. Since I've had them I've finally started thinking about what it is to be a bird… or to be anything, if you see what I mean."

Adrian didn't say anything.

"I wonder if they're happy or hungry or pissed off or feel claustrophobic and all caged up and stuff."

"They look pretty happy to me."

"I try to put myself in their shoes – except they don't wear shoes – and try to feel what they feel. Of course I know I can't just like 'know' what anybody's feeling. But I try which I think is probably enough…kind of…because there's no other possibility."

Adrian looked at her with his melting chocolate eyes. He knew she was sensitive from their two walks together and her pointing out things he had never looked at before, like how the color of buildings changed depending on what time of day it was.

"I see what you mean," he said.

"What really gets me is the thought that one day they will die and what will their life have been? A couple years in a cage in my apartment…"

"Maybe that's a good life for a bird."

"Maybe. At least the guy in the pet store said one's a male and the other's a female, so they at least might get to make some whoopie. Are you sure you don't want any orange juice or anything?"

"No, that's okay."

"Since you've lived in Lausanne all your life, why don't we go for a walk and you show me all your favorite places in the city."

"It's kind of cold out there."

"I've got plenty of clothes."

"Well... okay."

Jenny excused herself a second and went into her room to put on a wool undershirt and a thick sweater. Adrian watched Caramel and Snickers flutter from bar to bar in the cage. He had no idea which was which.

First they walked down the Avenue d'Ouchy. They both had wool hats and mittens on. They went up the Avenue d'Elysee and cut across through the school to the park that used to be the Queen of Spain's house and is now a photography museum. The museum wasn't open yet. They sat down on a bench and looked at the lake and Adrian asked Jenny where she thought she'd be in twenty years.

"Alive, I hope," Jenny said.

"Where do you want to live?"

"I haven't met many places I didn't like."

"Could you live in Lausanne?"

"Of course. Or Paris. Or San Francisco. Or Munich. Or Hong Kong."

"Have you been to Hong Kong?"

"No."

It was cold on the bench so they started walking again. They went downhill to the bottom of the park, turned left and took the small path behind the Beau Rivage Hotel over to the Olympic Museum. Here the view was even better and there were sculptures all over the place and views and sculptures always look better when you're in love.

They walked down to the lake and over to an old tower that is still half alive. The lake was silver and flat like the sky, only shinier. Then they walked through the Denantou Park where there was a big stone statue of a big naked woman with big breasts that wouldn't last five minutes in Salt Lake City without someone covering her up. That's what Jenny told Adrian anyway.

When they got to the north end of the park it started snowing lightly. Adrian said his next favorite place was the area around the cathedral which would mean walking all the way up the hill through the city. This was fine with Jenny. Her father had taught her to walk because when you walk you see more.

When a snowflake landed on Jenny's nose, Adrian flipped it off. The flakes were getting larger as the sky got closer.

In town, at the Place St. François, the Saturday market was in full swing. They meandered through the crowd to the Place de Palud where the Hotel de Ville was. Then Jenny followed Adrian up the covered wooden steps to the cathedral. They went inside and when Adrian asked Jenny if she believed in God she said, "Which one?" Adrian said, "The Christmas one," and Jenny said "I'd say the odds were about one in a million, but the church is nice."

When they came outside Adrian asked if she wanted a hot chocolate or anything and she said not yet, so they went back behind the cathedral and up the road to the Sauveblin Park. This was another kilometer uphill. Jenny had never been there. In the middle of a forest was a lake and a fenced area with deer, pigs, cows, and peacocks. The lake was frozen on some of the edges. Jenny told Adrian his eyes were the same color as the cows'.

They walked back down through the forest to the park that houses the Hermitage Museum. Adrian said he had never realized how many trees there were in Lausanne. Jenny took his hand.

It was almost twelve o'clock. The cafe next to the museum was open so this is where they had their hot chocolate and this was where they stared at each other goo-goo-eyed and talked about things for two hours. While they were talking Jenny wondered if a few years later she would remember anything they talked about. She thought about when she read "Anna Karenina" and now she couldn't remember one single conversation Anna had had with her lover. She just remembered the feeling.

Jenny and Adrian left the cafe as the snow was starting to stick on the ground. They kept each other from falling when the sidewalk got steep. It was a forty-five-minute walk back to Jenny's apartment where Jenny made them two cheese sandwiches with pickles and mustard. By then they were warm and they went in Jenny's bedroom and looked at a few pictures of Jenny in America with her mother and father. Then Jenny pulled her sweater over her head and then her undershirt and she didn't have a bra on. Adrian would remember that moment forever. But he wouldn't remember how his clothes came off or how it all happened or felt under the covers. Jenny would remember Adrian's chocolate eyes in the light that came through the silver window. When it got dark they didn't turn on a light until it was time for Adrian to go home.

16)

That really is pretty much how it went. Of course I don't know what Cherif will remember about the day, but when I took my sweater and undershirt off and was sitting there on the bed, he stopped looking at the pictures and stared at me with those chocolate eyes until I thought they were going to pop out of his pretty head. It's been more than a month now and we still have the hots for each other. During Christmas vacation we went skiing a couple of times up in Leysin, taking the train up in the morning and back again at night. Daddy likes Cherif a lot and even said he could sleep over on New Year's Eve, but Cherif said his mother would shoot him if he did. But he did stay until three in the morning. His mother is pretty nice, but I think she's afraid that I might get pregnant or something and she doesn't want him to get tied down or me to have an abortion or that kind of thing. Of course not spending the night together is no guarantee of anything because if people really want to get it on, they'll find a way and a time and a place. Especially in today's world. I don't think she knows that we have already done it about twenty times and that we're very careful about Cherif dressing in his best condom and everything. Cherif says his mother is afraid he'll end up being like his dad which, according to Cherif, means that he'll "eat a few grapes and end up being an alcoholic". Daddy just keeps telling me that life is short and to enjoy it while I can, but just to not do anything too dumb along the way. He trusts me enough, I think, to know what "too dumb" means.

Since this is really my first true love kind of thing, I'm trying to soak it all in slowly and not get too crazy or anything. I've read enough books – and Daddy's told me enough stories – about people thinking love will last forever and it never does, except for maybe one in every million rolls of the dice. The problem is the first love hits you like a tidal wave and it's hard not to drown. What I notice most is how you think so much about the other person that when you think about yourself you're still thinking about the other person. I mean you start seeing yourself through the other person's eyes. In some ways that kind of sucks because I can tell that if I'm not careful I'll end up being more of a slave than a girlfriend. I've mentioned this to Cherif and he says he knows exactly what I'm talking about, but he wonders if you can really control that kind of thing. I say if you don't control it you're looking for trouble somewhere up or down the line. I mean it can be even simple stuff like deciding which sweater to put on. Before I met Cherif I'd put on any old stupid sweater I wanted to put on; now I always think I should put on the sweater he wants me to put on. Of course he's not the type to be telling me what to wear or anything, but I know he likes some things better than others. Daddy says that that's one of the few good things about getting old… you don't give a flying rubber duck what other people think about what you're wearing or how your hair looks or if they like you or not. Anyway, my guess is that most people who are in love probably spent about three-quarters of their time worrying about what the other person is thinking about them and I've decided if that starts happening to me, I'm going to grab a parachute and jump out of the love jet….

The other thing I can tell could screw everything up is thinking about what Cherif is thinking about other girls. Imagine if I'm already worried about what he's thinking about me and then I start worrying about what he's thinking about Deborah or Elodie or Melissa or Lisa – all the other cuties at school – then I'm really going to chop myself to pieces. Daddy says jealousy is the poison in all love soups and I think he's right. The first time we talked about it was way before I met Cherif. I remember telling Daddy that I thought being jealous was just a way of showing the other person how much you loved them, and Daddy said, no, it was a way of showing the other person how much you didn't love yourself. I said don't bullshit me Daddy and he said wait until you fall in love then tell me about it. So since I've been in love I realize that every time I feel insecure and slightly jealous and crap it is because I'm not feeling so hot about myself… Anyway, love isn't all that simple, but so far so good. More or less.

One thing that isn't so good is that at school I don't spend nearly as much time messing around with my other friends as I did before. Now every time we have recess or a break I meet Cherif. We hold hands and look into each other's eyes and sneak in a little kiss every now and then, but all this time we're not with our other friends. Of course we've talked about keeping our own freedom to be with other people, but it's like there's a magnet that pulls us together whenever we're within a hundred meters of each other. I told Daddy this at dinner last night and he said, "Time will take care of that." I guess he means when the fire starts to burn down I'll start spreading myself a little thinner. Daddy was kind of in a weird mood though last night. I know he's happy that I'm happy and all that, but I think sometimes he's not so happy himself. I know teaching at the business school has become a rather royal pain in the ass, but he's only going to teach one more year before he retires. He says that business is like religion… it's addictive and is mostly a reflection of the make-up of the human head. He says it's all about wanting the goodies and once you have them, wanting more. Animals are different. They couldn't care less about the next life and they're not all crazy for the goodies in this life. They just want enough to get them through to tomorrow or to the end of the winter. Daddy says people are pretty much wasting their time…. They accumulate far too much crap in this life and the odds are that there is no next life…. Last night at the end of our conversation Daddy was a little drunk on his wine and he said that everything felt "superfluous". Actually he said the only thing that didn't feel superfluous was me. Before I went to bed I looked "superfluous" up in the Big Fat Red book just to be sure I knew what he meant. It made me kind of sad and happy at the same time.

What's funny about Daddy is that even though he's a teacher of business he hardly ever buys anything except groceries. I mean business is all about making stuff, selling stuff, and consuming stuff and Daddy does none of the three. He stopped buying new clothes years ago (maybe a pair of shoes once in a while when an old one has a hole in the sole), he drives the same car that he first got when we came to Switzerland, he doesn't wear a watch, and he doesn't even have a cell phone. When I asked him how you can teach at a business school and not have a cell phone he said, "It's easy when there's nobody you want to talk to." I told him to stop bullshitting and he said, "Except my daughter, and I see her every night." I guess he's kind of like a priest and an atheist at the same time, or maybe a psychiatrist who knows all along that he's the one who's crazy. But in Daddy's case I'd say it's more like the opposite.

17)

Can somebody tell me if the fad of everybody sticking earphones in their ears and headphones on their heads all the time will ever go away? When I say my prayers at night I say "DEAR HOLY ALMIGHTY GREAT SILENT GOD WHOEVER AND WHEREVER YOU ARE BE IT IN THE SINGULAR OR PLURAL, PLEASE BLESS THE WORLD THAT THERE WILL BE NO MORE EARTHQUAKES IN HAITI AND CHILE AND NO MORE TSUNAMIS IN ASIA AND NO MORE STARVATION IN AFRICA AND THAT ALL THE IPODS WILL DISAPPEAR FROM THE FACE OF THE EARTH AND PEOPLE WILL LISTEN TO BIRDS CHIRP AGAIN INSTEAD OF ALL THIS HIP-HOP SHIT AND WHATEVER OTHER MIND-DEADENING ELECTRONS ARE SHOOTING THROUGH MY FRIENDS' EARS INTO THEIR BRAINS. I'm so sick of this obsession with music all the time that I want to throw up. Even Cherif does it sometimes. He just doesn't do it ALL the time like most of the kids in my school. Today we had an English test the last period of school and even though there is a rule at school that you cannot have iPods or iPhones or other electronic devices in class, everybody is always trying to listen to music by sliding the wires up their shirts and through their sleeves and hiding the earphones by pulling their hair in front of their ears or putting their hands over them, etc. etc. ...anyway, today the English teacher says, "All right all you music-crazed youth of Switzerland, I have decided that the school rule for no iPods and other musical devices is counterproductive to your brilliant educations. So, when you finish your test today you CAN LISTEN quietly to whatever you want to. JUST SHUT UP AND DON'T TALK and DON'T TELL THE DIRECTOR OR ANY OTHER TEACHERS I LET YOU DO IT!!!" So when kids handed in their tests they all had their music in their pockets and they all put it in their ears and it was the first time all the kids stayed totally quiet while the others were finishing their tests. Usually the ones who turn in their tests are all excited and try to talk to each other and distract the other kids who are still working. Today everybody shut up and sat there like drugged-up angels listening to their music. At the end of the class the English teacher said he was going to propose a new school rule that kids who don't want to work can listen to music so they will shut up and let the others who want to work work. He said he was serious. I think there are only about three kids in the whole damn school who don't have an iPod or whatever and I'm one of them. I guess this is Daddy's influence, but so what? Why do kids want to spend half their lives listening to music and playing stupid games on their phones. Actually the truth is I did have one of those little Nintendos when I was about six years old and one day I got so sick of pecking the keys and losing dumb games that I threw it out of the window while Daddy was driving the car. This was in America where it's even worse. Daddy stopped the car (we were out in the country going to some place like Napa Valley where Daddy used to stock up on his drug...wine) and he said that either I had to walk back and get it or we'd leave it where it was, but if I didn't go get it, he would never buy me another one. I left it.

Anyway, it's pretty funny how the English teacher used the music obsession to his advantage and we had the quietest test in the history of the class. But I still don't get this obsession with music, music, music, music.... Daddy says it's a fad pushed on the consumer-slaves by the likes of Sony and Apple because they have to keep inventing new and better stuff so that all the drug addicts will buy new and better junk so Sony and Apple won't go out of business... which is exactly what happens.... Walkman becomes iPod... iPod becomes iPhone... iPhone becomes iPad... iPad becomes iFad... and on and on to keep the earth turning.... Maybe I'm the one who's crazy because I don't listen to music all the time, but I'd rather listen to Snickers and Caramel chirp. Daddy listens to classical stuff, but not all the time.

Speaking of Snickers and Caramel... up until two days ago there were three plastic bars in their cage that they'd jump around on from one to the other. These bars kept falling down every time we'd open the cage to do something. So Daddy got some real branches from real trees and cut them to the right length and put two of them where the two bottom plastic ones were. He left the plastic one on top where they sleep. Since he did this, Caramel refuses to sit on the new branches. She flies from the top perch directly to the food bowl on the side of the cage. Normally she stops on the branch near the food bowl, then hops into the food bowl from there. But now she refuses – absolutely refuses – to land on the new branch! And it's a REAL branch. I mean a REAL TREE branch. Not a PLASTIC branch. My guess is that she got used to the smooth plastic and doesn't like the feel of the rough wood on her little feet…. But who knows? Snickers will land on any branch. But not Caramel. Maybe one of her ancestors had a traumatic experience with a branch and it got passed on in her bird genes. I only thought of this because maybe it reminded me of my refusal of all the new music devices that everybody plugs into their ears. For whatever reason, (Daddy's genes maybe) I refuse….

18)

Daddy is getting worse. Well, sort of. Since he told me the whole world felt superfluous, I've noticed he's drinking more wine at night. Actually I kind of don't mind because I really do like sitting at the dinner table and talking because when all is said and done, Daddy is kind of my best friend. I mean when you think of everything we've been through together, like Mommy dying and moving to Europe together and both learning to speak French and figuring things out here in Switzerland and all, it makes sense that we've become closer than most fathers and daughters. But last night he made this delicious little pork roast with potatoes, carrots, onions, and garlic, and he kept nibbling at it and sipping wine and we kept talking and finally the next thing you know, he had finished the whole bottle of wine. He said it was the best Swiss merlot he'd ever drunk. (I don't know the difference between a merlot and a pinus noir – lol – but that doesn't matter…) I know it's none of my business how much wine Daddy drinks, but he usually has half a bottle or maybe three-quarters at the most. But last night he downed the whole bottle like it was Kool-Aid (I wonder if Kool-Aid even exists anymore…). It's really not just the wine, but he doesn't seem to laugh as much as he used to. Or if he does laugh, he just chuckles and the next second he's rubbing his forehead or something. Plus he told me at the end of the pork roast that for the first time in his life, when he looks at all the cute secretaries at the business school, he doesn't think any more about a little "roll in the hay", but to the contrary, feels like "the electric organ's not plugged in". I've always thought that people being horny was a good sign because it was a sign of life, vitality, being alive and all that, and Daddy's present state kind of confirms my idea in reverse. His horns seem to have all fallen off and he doesn't want to chase those pink panties anymore.

The other thing was that after the bottle of wine he had a glass of cognac which he never does, except on Christmas or his birthday or something. I guess I should see if it keeps going on or gets worse or whatever before I get too excited, but you've got to understand that he is my daddy, I don't have a mommy or a brother or sister, and I'm not seventeen years old yet. Plus, I love the guy, if you know what I mean….

Speaking of love, it's been six weeks since Daddy went to Budapest, since Cherif and I had our walk through Lausanne, since Cherif and I made real love in my nice warm bed after eating our cheese sandwiches. I guess I should stop counting the weeks, but every Saturday I get reminded of it all like it happened yesterday. Today Cherif has a rugby game in Sion and will be gone all day. When he plays in Lausanne I usually go and watch, but they don't let fans go on the bus with them when they go on long trips (not that Sion is a "long" trip – it's only an hour away, but for people in Switzerland it's like driving from San Francisco to Los Angeles). Cherif says the coach thinks that fans on the bus would be a "distraction". My guess is that a "distraction" is probably exactly what the players need so they're not all nervous and everything before a game. But what do I know? Actually it's fine with me that they won't let groupies on the bus, because the truth is rugby bores me to death. I think it's even more boring than soccer which I used to think was the most boring game in the world, except for ice hockey, basketball, tennis, and American football. All of which means I'm not a great sports fan. But I am a fan of watching Cherif (and, I must admit, a couple of the other guys on his team) run around in those shorts and cute red socks up to the knees and the cute little shirt with the shoulder pads. Plus I like the way Cherif's dreadlocks fly around and get all smashed up when he plays. After about five minutes of the game, he usually starts looking like an old teddy bear that's been chewed up by a mob of dogs, which only makes him cuter. There's one guy on the team who doesn't have big muscles, but who kind of lopes like an antelope when he runs and is fun to watch too. Otherwise, rugby makes about as much sense to me as a Chinese crossword puzzle.

So today I won't see Cherif for one single second which Daddy says is good for me. He has invited me to go "raquette" walking up in the Jura mountains, which is really one of the coolest things I've done in years. I guess "raquette" is just the French word for snowshoe, but since we lived around San Francisco where there wasn't ever any snow, snowshoes were never a major part of my existence.... Anyway, Daddy and I did it for the first time right after Christmas because Santa Claus gave us both a shiny new pair of raquettes. Mine are red and Daddy's are blue. You just put them on any old walking boots and start walking in the snow. What's great is that you can walk absolutely anywhere with them and you don't sink too far in soft snow or slip and slide on ice. The first time we went to a place called Marchairuz which has this incredible view of Mt. Blanc (the highest mountain in Europe) and all the Alps. It was a perfect day and everybody we met walking acted like they were having a two-hour orgasm or something because everything was so beautiful... which I must say, it was.

Today Daddy wants to go to another area in the Jura called Mollendruz which is not far away, just behind the town of Cossonay. Today it's kind of cloudy and might even snow, but we're going anyway. This winter of 2010 has been colder than a witch's left tit, which is kind of ironic given how Al Gore is beating everybody's brain with pictures of polar bear ice chunks melting and all that crap. I wish Gore had pictures from sixty-five million years ago when all the dinosaurs got wiped off the face of the earth. I wonder whose fault that was? I read an article the other day in the newspaper saying the dinosaurs and lots of other darling little creatures got snuffed because a meteor about ten miles long smashed into Mexico causing the earth to go crazy for a while. What a world! Anyway, this is the coldest winter Switzerland has had in decades…. Daddy likes the raquette walking too because his says his knee doesn't feel so hot and he's kind of afraid to ski on it. I hope it gets better because our trips to places like Zermatt are some of my favorite memories of living here. Another time we went to Wengen which also has no cars and they also have a train that takes you up to ten thousand feet so you don't even have to ride a chairlift if you don't want to. These villages are so quaint and beautiful with all their old chalets and fountains and hand carvings on everything. If we ever move back to America, I'll really miss them… which makes me think… there's not really one thing I miss in America anymore. When I first got here I missed everything so much I wanted to cry every five minutes, but little by little all that disappeared. Daddy says the same thing. The other kids are cool, the weather's cool (I like the four seasons), it's good to know another language like French, you don't have traffic jams all over the place like in the Bay Area, you don't have to always get in a car to go anywhere (I walk across the street to a grocery store), there are seven cinemas within five minutes of my house (one is porno, but we'll count it anyway), the lake is five minutes away, and the center of town is eight minutes from my door… all on foot! The other thing that's great is that all these other countries are just a short train or plane ride away... France, Spain, Italy, Austria, Germany, Hungary, Greece, Turkey, Morocco, Tunisia, England, Ireland, Belgium, Holland etc. Damn, the more I think about it, the more I like it here! And Daddy has promised to take me to Morocco for Easter vacation....

Speaking of Daddy, he's calling me asking if I'm ready to go. I am. I just have to turn this machine off and put my boots on. Walking in the snow with Daddy is almost as good as sitting in a hot bath when we get home... Now I'm the one who's bullshitting. The bath would be nothing without the walk.

19)

Speaking of Al Gore… could this be true? You read it and tell me. A friend sent me the online link to it today:

Tale of Two Houses

House Number 1:
A 20-room mansion (not including 8 bathrooms) heated by natural gas. Add on a pool (and a pool house) and separate guest house, all heated by gas. In one month this residence consumes more energy than the average American household does in a year. The average bill for electricity and natural gas runs over $2,400 per month. In natural gas alone, this property consumes between 12 and 20 times more than the national average for an American home. This home is not situated in a Northern or Midwestern "snow belt" area. It's in the South.

House Number 2:
Designed by an architecture professor at a leading national university. This house incorporates every "green" feature current home construction can provide. The house is 4,000 square feet (4 bedrooms) and is nestled on a high prairie in the American Southwest. A central closet in the house holds geothermal heat pumps

drawing ground water through pipes that sink 300 feet into the ground. The water (usually 67 degrees) heats the house in the winter and cools it in the summer. The system uses no fossil fuel such as oil or natural gas and it consumes one-quarter of the electricity required for a conventional heating/cooling system. Rainwater from the roof is collected and funneled into a 25,000 gallon underground cistern. Wastewater from showers, sinks, and toilets goes into underground purifying tanks and then into the cistern. The collected water then irrigates the land surrounding the house. Surrounding flowers and shrubs native to the area enable the property to blend into the surrounding landscape.

<u>House Number 1</u> is outside Nashville, Tennessee; it is the abode of the "environmentalist" Al Gore.

<u>House Number 2</u> is on a ranch near Crawford, Texas; it is the residence of ex-President of the United States, George W. Bush.

An "inconvenient truth".

So, if this is true it's pretty funny and if it's not true it's pretty cruel, if you see what I mean. That's the problem with the internet. You can make anybody look like a total fool or the coolest thing on earth... That's why when I rag on somebody, I really don't mean it too seriously, because deep down inside I know I don't really have any idea what the truth is or what the person is really like. Especially if it's a person I've never even met like Al Gore. Just the other day this teacher in school starts telling us that September 11 was really not Al Qaida's doing, but was an inside job done by Bush and the C.I.A. He said if you look at all the "facts" on the internet (where else do people look for "facts" these days?), you can see that it was impossible for two airplanes to bring down the Twin Towers like they did and that only the "extra explosives" planted inside the buildings had made it possible for the whole mess to take place. He kept talking about "fact" this and "fact" that. When I told him I really didn't think Bush and his cronies would do such a thing, he said I was naïve. He said that he wasn't the only one who believed this, but that little by little the "truth" was coming out and that now probably half the teachers in the school believed it…. What I'm trying to say is that the new God of Nature, HRH INTERNET, can get people to believe ANYTHING….

So I don't know if Al Gore is a nice guy or the biggest phoniest asshole ever to hit the American political scene (which might potentially be confirmed by his haircut). Don't forget that he won the Nobel Peace Prize. So, if he is a big phony, then that means that the Nobel Peace Prize people are either extremely dumb or a bunch of phonies themselves. One thing I do know is that when Al Gore came to the University of Lausanne a couple of years ago to show his movie and talk, a friend of Daddy's, the ex-head of the Engineering School, said he was kind of a pompous turd who got paid tons of money for a lousy speech. Hey, maybe Bush is a turd like all the Europeans think (95% anyway…Daddy told me that the day Obama got elected, he was sitting with a bunch of European friends and he asked them if they had anything good to say about Bush. Zero. Not one nice word. Then he asked them if they had anything bad to say about Obama. Zero. Not one bad word. Daddy says that just goes to show you what the media can do. And now Obama's starting to get the same treatment as Bush). Daddy did tell me once that he'd rather have lunch with Bush than Gore because at least Bush has a sense of humor and doesn't take himself too seriously. But hey, the odds are we're probably all full of "merde" most of the time…

Before I forget, I have to give you the latest on me and Cherif. The Monday after his rugby match in Sion (they won easily and he made all kinds of touchdowns or whatever you call it when you go across the goal line), he came over after school and we had our first argument. For some reason his breath smelled bad and when he started kissing me on the bed I kind of pulled away and when he asked me what was wrong I said I didn't know, which of course was a lie. Then after I thought about it for a couple of seconds I thought why shouldn't I tell him that his breath smelled bad, so I did. He asked me if it was the first time and I said more or less. He didn't like that either because he said it meant that he had had bad breath before but I hadn't told him which meant that there were times before when I hadn't enjoyed kissing him. I said everybody gets bad breath once in a while and that it's no big deal. He said I never had bad breath which made me feel kind of good, so I just told him to go in the bathroom and brush his teeth with my toothbrush and then we could get down to business (I didn't use those exact words, but we hadn't been alone together for four days…). He went into the bathroom and brushed his teeth, but when he came back he just sat on the bed looking all sad and everything like his dreadlocks were going to fall out or like all the air had been taken out of his basketball shoes. I kissed him on the neck a few times, but that didn't help. To make a short story shorter, I finally went right to the old fire hose and eventually that got a reaction and we got undressed and played under the covers and everything. But, the truth is the whole thing lacked our normal passion. It was like we were acting and not doing, if you see what I mean. Actually to say we had an argument isn't really accurate. It was more like we had our first "downer". It was the first time things hadn't been fun and exciting and full of genuine fireworks. He knew it and I knew it and he felt lousy and I felt lousy. The next day at school, which was yesterday, we pretended like nothing had happened, but you could tell things weren't all hunky-dory, like when you go to a party and you're supposed to be having fun but you'd really rather be home reading a book or watching TV. I guess this kind of thing must happen to everybody, I mean everybody who's ever been in love. So what do you do? You forget it and move on, right? I mean if you can't get over a little thing like a couple nostrils full of bad breath, imagine trying to raise children together! Did I say I want children? Actually, I think I do want children – for one reason. I want to be a mommy like daddy is a daddy. When he told me the only true true love in the world is between a parent and a child I'm starting to wonder if he wasn't right, and if he was, I don't want to miss out on being the parent part of the equation. I guess I'm just not sure now if Cherif would make the right daddy. Of course I wonder if my great relationship with Daddy is because of all we went through together with Mommy and of course I wouldn't want my own husband to have to die in order to have a stellar relationship with my own kid, etc... But maybe if Mommy hadn't died tragically Daddy and I would just have a normal father-daughter relationship, whatever that means... (There is probably no such thing as a "normal" father-daughter relationship any more than there is such a thing as a "normal" tomato or a "normal" belly button or a "normal" childhood or a "normal" car accident. Everything only happens just once to whomever it's happening to. So if nothing happens the same way twice, then saying something is "normal" is like saying a guy who lives in a gas heated 20-room mansion is an "environmentalist". Sometimes I can't believe how full of baloney everybody is....)

It's time for bed. I'm reading Anna Karenina for the second time. I started it the other day when I remembered how Anna and her boyfriend (Count Vronsky or whatever his name is) were kind of like me and Cherif – I mean all head-over-heels for each other – and then I remembered how the whole thing finally went sour in the end and she ended up jumping in front of a train. I just wanted to check it out in case I start thinking about jumping in front of a train. But deep down inside I don't think that's my style. Plus, Anna felt guilty about all kinds of things and if there's one thing in this world Daddy has taught me it's to do what I think is right and not mess myself up feeling guilty about crap.

20)

These chapters are starting to fly by. I can't believe I'm on Chapter Twenty. But I guess it all depends on how long the chapters are. Some books are eight hundred pages and have no chapters. When you think about it, what are chapters for? Nothing, except a pause or a break like recess at school.

But that's not what I want to talk about. What I want to talk about is two things: being blind and being a rhinoceros. They don't really go together, but in my case they sort of do. The other day I made friends with a blind woman whose parents live just two buildings over from us. She is really blind blind, like Stevie Wonder blind. Some blind people can make out shapes and things, but she can't see anything. She has a dog for eyes and one of those white sticks she pokes around in front of her. I met her when I was going down to the bakery yesterday evening to get a dessert for Daddy. He's not a big dessert guy, but I know every now and then he loves a nice little chocolate cake or something. And I know he's still kind of in a "bored with 99% of life" phase, so I thought I'd get him a dessert for after the spaghetti I was making.

Anyway, it's about six o'clock and I'm walking down the sidewalk seeing cars and trees and people and everything and suddenly this blind woman coming my way drops her grocery bag. The dog stops and starts sniffing around and she gets down on one knee and starts feeling around for things. A couple of oranges and cans of stuff had fallen out and rolled away. By this time I was right next to her, so I asked her if I could help her and she heard my accent and asked me where I was from. I told her America and she said she once knew a man from America that she used to give massages to when she was younger and going to massage school (I guess when you think about it, it's true… you don't have to see to give a good massage. People in love are massaging each other in the dark all the time…) and that he was a really nice guy and all, which obviously had nothing to do with me, but maybe she hadn't met another American since then. Anyway, I picked up all her stuff for her and she stood there holding her bag and stick and dog leash and my guess is that she kind of forgot exactly where she was and how many steps she had taken and all that because she just stood there kind of moving her lips without saying anything. I asked her if I could help her go where she was going and she said she was going to Boulevard de Grancy number 18 and that it was not far. I told her I lived at number 14 and that I'd be happy to walk her there. She said it wasn't necessary, but when I insisted a little she accepted. So for about seventy meters walking down the sidewalk with her, for the first time in my whole dumb life, I think I kind of actually had a small feeling for what it was like to be blind. As we were walking and I was holding on to her elbow, I actually shut my eyes a couple of times for a few seconds. We were going pretty slowly and I only did it when nobody was coming in our direction. What really shocked me was that as soon as I shut my eyes I started hearing all the noises around us in the street. Up until then I hadn't noticed a single solitary noise, because it's the same noise I hear all the time that I'm so used to that I don't "hear" anymore. It made me think that blind people probably kind of "see" with their ears…. Anyway, it turns out that she was going to visit her parents (she has a small apartment a couple blocks away) who now are pretty old. We said goodbye at the door in front of the building because she thanked me at that point and I could tell she wanted to go the rest of the way alone. What got me about the whole thing was that I suddenly realized I had seen lots of blind people and seen the movie on Ray Charles and everything, but never had I really felt what blind people live. Not that I do now, but at least the word "blind" took on a different meaning…

… Just like the word "rhinoceros" did today… When Daddy and I first came to Switzerland he always had the radio on in the apartment because he said if we listened to French all the time we'd learn it without even trying. I told him he was full of angel shit, but it turns out he was kind of right. (He said, "How do you think babies learn a language?" and I guess I was too dumb to see what he meant.) So I got in the habit of listening to the radio all the time – not the junk music stations, but more the talk show stuff. After school today I was listening to this old French woman talk about a book she wrote that takes place way back (not so "way back" if you think about it) in the 16th century – she said something about "the crusades" – and she talked about a guy from India giving a king in Europe (Spain or Portugal I think) a rhinoceros for a present. I mean I know today presidents and prime ministers give each other koala bears and pandas and stuff, but imagine giving somebody a rhino back in the 16th century!!! Imagine transporting the thing!!! I'm so dumb it had never occurred to me that rhinos even existed five hundred years ago. I kind of thought they were made by zoo people so we could see them in zoos... Anyway, you get my point. Imagine what it means to be a rhinoceros. Imagine what it meant five hundred years ago to get captured in India or Africa or somewhere and get transported on a boat to Europe. Imagine all the food it ate and all the rhino poop somebody had to clean up on the boat. And imagine what was going through the rhino's head when all this was happening! I mean it was probably bad enough for Snickers and Caramel spending an hour in those little boxes with slits on the sides when we first brought them home, but imagine the months that rhino spent in some dark corner of a boat probably with its legs chained to the wall! I can't. It all kind of started to make me go crazy and I started thinking about dinosaurs and buffalos and elephants and worms and mosquitos and jellyfish and guppies and hippies, not to speak of blind people and deaf people and crippled people and dumb people and ugly people and beautiful people and snakes and chickens and amoebas and viruses and camels and Californians and Japanese and turtles and birds.... And then I started thinking about all the zillions of animals and plants and people that had died and disintegrated in the crust of the earth and were now just "fossil fuel" or dust or...nothing! It made me want to call Cherif and have a party or make love or something!

But Daddy came home to rescue me. He liked the chocolate dessert. He also drank a whole bottle of Chianti wine.

21)

I don't know why I keep writing "Chapter this" and "Chapter that". Who cares? I guess since this is my first real book I wanted to imitate "Anna Karenina" or "The Grapes of Wrath" and have chapters because chapters are what Tolstoy and Steinbeck do. Maybe I'll just finish the book with no more chapters. What are they really good for? I guess they're just like going to bed at night… a break. You could say the same about paragraphs and punctuation. But when you think about it there's really no break from birth to death. Even if you go in a coma or something, you're still there and you have to deal with whatever is going on around you. I mean breaks are always kind of artificial if you see what I mean. Even when you tell yourself to not do anything, you're still doing something. Everything is really all smashed together, cradle to grave, but we do our best to make it look like it isn't….

Anyway, what I want to say now goes with what was in Chapter Twenty because it has to do with another interview I heard on the radio this morning. This one was with a nineteen-year-old feminist – that's what she called herself – about the condition of women. What really got me was how she kept comparing the condition of women to the condition of men and implying how women were still somehow inferior to "men", as if "men" were the measure of all things. Maybe if she compared the state of women to eagles or lions or flowers, I could understand what she was saying, but MEN! From what I can see, most men are all pretty screwed up and for a woman to want to be like them or compare herself to them doesn't make any sense at all. She started giving statistics for jobs after college. I mean what job is really a good job? Being the manager of a bank? Running a shoe store? Being Secretary of Commerce? How about bodyguard for Tom Cruise? Cleaning toilets at the airport? Lawyer? Teacher? Pinup? Photographer of pinups? I mean really, come on everybody, who's to say what's a good job or a bad job? Who's to say what a good life or a bad life is? What's a good way to spend your time in this world? Maybe a woman carrying a basket on her head in Ethiopia is living a far better life than some businessman who's all worried about his tan or how many millions he's got in the bank and if he should get a Ferrari instead of a Mercedes. Wanting to be like that man is like wanting to be like an asshole and what woman in her right mind would want to be an asshole? From what Daddy tells me I sure wouldn't want to be like most of his fellow professors at the Business School. He says they spent the first part of their lives trying to get rich and now they're spending the last part teaching others how to get rich. If you're spending your time trying to get rich, think of all the other things you're NOT doing that might be a whole lot more worthwhile... like being an eagle cruising through the sky or a cat purring next to a fireplace.

Of course I'm not talking about feminists complaining about getting raped or getting screwed on their salary or anything. That's as obvious as a full moon. No, I'm talking about women – people actually – taking two minutes to step back and look at what counts as cool in our culture and then really asking themselves, "Is this what I want out of this life?" I have time to think about this all day in school because most of what's going on is so boring, and the more I think about it the more I think both men and women are pretty dumb... men for all the garbage they strive for and women for comparing themselves to some pretty lowly creatures. I tried to imagine what this nineteen-year-old girl would be saying had she been born a boy. What would be her line then? Maybe she'd be a football coach or something and be talking about how to win football games! But I know I'll never be a feminist because there aren't many men or women I see who are living lives I'd like to imitate or even resemble in the slightest way.

Speaking of resembling in the slightest way... the other day a kid brought in a DVD about life in the ghetto in America – in the film they called it "living in the hood". He asked the English teacher if we could watch it on Friday afternoon when we always watch a film because everybody's too excited and crazy to do anything else. The teacher said okay as long as the film wasn't for 18-year-olds meaning it had so much sex and violence in it that it would dirty our minds. Of course most kids' minds are already totally filthy because of all the junk on the internet, but that's another problem. The teacher read the cover and it was supposedly suitable for 12-year-olds in today's world. In ancient Rome it probably would have been suitable for gladiators.... Anyway, the teacher put it on and started correcting some tests. The film was sort of a comedy, but every sentence had about five motherfuckers and fucks in it and there were all kinds of drive-by shootings and fights and everybody insulting each other all the time. All this is mixed with the cool rap music that everybody listens to. I thought, "This is the model for the kids in the ghettos of America?" How did civilization ever get to such a point?

I sat there and watched the kids around me watching it. They were the most concentrated they've been all year (remember the fight between Abdul and Jerome during "Titanic"?). They were totally quiet except for when they'd laugh at stuff like a guy punching an old woman in the face or a guy shooting a machine gun from his crotch. It turns out almost all the kids had already seen the film, too. It was like reciting the Pledge of Allegiance or the Ten Commandments when Daddy was a kid. This stuff was built into their brains. The teacher got up from his desk a couple of times to watch and I could tell he kind of felt like I did, but I think he was just happy the kids were quiet so that he could correct his dumb tests.

Actually, now that I think about it, last week Cherif took me to see a movie called "Inglorious Bastards" that is up for an Academy Award for Best Picture. Well, if it wins, the world is really in trouble. I couldn't believe the violence. In fact I closed my eyes half the time after the scene where they cut the top of guys' heads off. Cherif says that it's just Tarataurantula's (his real name is something like Tarantino) way of showing what mankind is all about. Which is exactly my point about the feminist stuff... why would anybody want to have anything to do with "man"kind, much less want to imitate him or have what he has? Except for maybe things like Mozart's 21st Piano Concerto or Monet (no relation to Marcel as far as I know) paintings or inventing the polio vaccination... but that's not what the 19-year-old feminist on the radio was talking about.

Forget the chapters. From now on I'll just skip a few spaces depending on my mood. Twenty-One chapters were plenty anyway.

It's already March and it's still winter around here. It keeps snowing all the time and it's minus 7 degrees centigrade every morning and the north wind (they call it "la bise") has been so strong lately that it knocked a bunch of trees down. But Swiss weather changes like Biden and Obama change ties. (We get CNN and every time I see the President or the Vice-President, they're wearing a different tie. Speaking of CNN...who looks dumber? The male commentators with their ironed shirts and their hair all perfectly in place or the female commentators with their wax faces and bottles of hairspray.) In another week or two it'll be sunny and the tulips will be popping out of their pots.

You're probably worried about Daddy. I am too, but not because he's drinking more wine. I'm worried about him because he'll be sixty-four-years-old tomorrow. Anybody who's sixty-four-years-old has plenty to worry about. Like Daddy says, when you think about it, there are so many things that can go wrong with a human body (just about any kind of "body" for that matter, except maybe celestial bodies like stars, but even they explode in a million pieces every now and then…) that it's almost a miracle anybody makes it to sixty-four… heart, eyes, nose, feet, joints, blood, liver, pancreas, intestines, colon, uterus, prostate, breasts, brain, lungs, muscles, tendons, ears, knees, elbows, ankles, neck, spine, disks, meniscus, thyroid, and on and on and on…. That's what I'm worried about with Daddy… not the wine. As long as he doesn't drink his wine and go crash the car and mess somebody up, it's fine with me. He almost always drinks it at home, or if we go to a restaurant we walk. Besides, Daddy says good wine is one of the finest things mankind has ever invented… so I guess he'd be pretty dumb not to take advantage of it! I went to a wine store after school today and got him his birthday present: a bottle of local merlot made by a guy named Monachon who the guy in the wine store said is the best merlot maker in the Canton de Vaud. Daddy always says he's got everything he needs and that he likes presents that he can consume that don't end up taking up space in a drawer or closet. So the last couple of years I've got him wine and he seems to appreciate it.

He loved the wine. He drank the whole bottle with his birthday dinner, except for the little taste he let me have. I made him a chicken dish with rice. Daddy says he digests chicken or pork much better than beef. We really don't eat much meat – which is fine with me – maybe once a week at the most. We're more pasta and salad people. I don't think Daddy got any other presents for his birthday which is kind of sad when you think about it. But he probably didn't tell any friends or anybody at his school what day it was. That's the way he is. I got him a really good little chocolate cake down at the patisserie shop – the one I got the dessert from when I met the blind woman – and put a few candles on it just to make it look like a birthday cake. There wouldn't haven't been room for sixty-four even if I'd tried....

... Speaking of the blind woman... I've been keeping an eye out for her but I haven't seen her again. I'm wondering if she still gives massages. She's probably about fifty now. There were a lot of things I wanted to talk to her about and I thought if she still gave massages, she could give me one and we'd have about forty-five minutes to talk about everything under the roof including what it's really like to be blind blind. The other thing I thought was that it would be really interesting to compare her hands on my body with Cherif's hands on my body. I wonder if it's two totally different feelings or if I shut my eyes maybe Cherif's hands and her hands would have the same effect... at least when they are on certain parts of my body. Of course Cherif spends most of his time around my boobs and between my legs, but sometimes he wanders to my arms, legs, stomach, back, and neck. If I see her again, at least I'm going to ask her...

While we were eating dinner Daddy asked me if I'd like to go to Marrakesh for Easter vacation. I'd love to go to Marrakesh... anytime! With all the talk about Islam here in Switzerland, I'd like to see a real Muslim country up close. In case you don't remember or don't read newspapers or listen to the news too much, the Swiss recently voted to ban building new minarets in their country, which is one of the funniest things I've ever heard because they can still build new synagogues, football stadiums, McDonald's restaurants, and Christian churches all over the place. Everybody says there's too much of a Muslim influence. What about too much of a

Catholic influence (with their priests molesting choir boys between tunes all over the place) or too much of a BigMac influence (with fat people popping up around here faster than tulips in spring) or too much of a football influence (all the hooligans running around breaking windows and people wasting half their lives watching dumb games on TV) etc. etc.… Or how about too much of a rap music influence or a violent film influence? When are they going to vote about that? I really do like Switzerland and all, but sometimes these people can be really dumber than doorbells that don't ring….

Anyway, I told Daddy to get those tickets to Marrakesh. While we were eating the birthday cake he told me about a friend of his who's about his age who used to come to the school every year and teach a class, but whom he hadn't seen for a while. She was the boss of a big company that hauls money around, Brinks or something. Anyway, Daddy said he also knew her husband who was the boss of a bunch of hospitals and that they looked like they were one of the happiest couples in the world and had been married for about ninety years and had raised two beautiful kids and had a big house with a garden and a swimming pool and on and on.… Well Daddy met her at the gas station a week ago and she didn't look so good and since he hadn't seen her for a while, he invited her to a cafe for a cup of coffee. She told him that six months ago her company suddenly told her she had to retire because of her age – she'd been the boss for a bunch of years, like seventeen or something – and then about a month after she'd been retired her husband told her he was leaving her for another woman who lived in Paris on the Champs Elysee or something. Daddy asked her if it was a younger woman and she said, "No, that's the crazy part." The woman was the same age as she was. So Daddy's point was that here was a woman who had been busy as a queen bee with her company who suddenly is told to retire, who then is told by her husband that he's retiring her too for a woman that she had never known about in Paris… and now she lives ALONE in her big house with a big garden and swimming pool with nothing but free time on her hands 24/7/365. Talk about life going from A to Z – or Z to A if you prefer – overnight. Daddy said he told me the story just to show me how it's probably not a good idea to ever put all your eggs in one basket even though in life it's hard not to do it. I guess he was subtly referring to how losing Mommy had been such a hard thing to overcome.

His friend – Beatrice was her name – almost had it worse in that Mommy didn't leave Daddy for another man and so he never wasted his time waiting for her to call or come back because she was dead and everything. Plus Daddy said he had me and his job whereas Beatrice had no more kids around, no more job, and a big empty house. He said he was going to invite her to dinner one night because she was such a nice person. Actually he said her husband was a really nice person too and that he learned long ago never to judge the life of a couple because one never knows what goes on behind closed doors and between open ears.

I met the blind woman today on my way home from school. She was walking down the Avenue d'Ouchy and I was walking up. She had her dog of course and when I stopped in front of her the dog stopped and she stopped. I guess she can feel the dog stops when the leash isn't pulling anymore. I said a couple of words and asked her if she remembered me and she said she almost never forgets a voice, especially ones with nice accents like mine. I didn't beat around the bush and asked her if she still gave massages and she said she hadn't for quite a while, but since I lived right next to her parents and she still had her massage table in her parents' spare bedroom, she'd be happy to give me one. She asked me how old I was and when I said sixteen her lips and eyes starting moving and she said she'd have to have some kind of permission from my parents, like a letter or something. I told her that would be absolutely no problem. She said maybe it would be best if we fixed a rendezvous right then and there. It's for Saturday morning at ten o'clock. Cherif and I were going to do something, like walk around the outdoor market up in the old town, but we can do that starting at eleven. I think the woman was really happy to have something on her agenda, though it's hard to be sure. After we said goodbye I started thinking about how it would be interesting to have an appointment to massage somebody when you had absolutely no idea what the person looked like or what kind of body he or she had. When Cherif massages me he knows exactly what he's getting into. The blind woman only knows that I'm a girl and I'm sixteen. I could be skinny as a table leg or fat as a pig... she won't know until her hands start moving around my body....

I told Cherif at school today about the massage rendezvous. If you want to know the truth he seemed a little jealous of the idea of having somebody else's paws crawling over my skin. He tried to be all cool and everything, but I could tell that deep down under his skin the idea wasn't meeting with unanimity. I tried to imagine how I'd feel if he told me that some blind guy was going to massage him on Saturday morning. I realized that the first thought I would have would be that the blind guy was probably gay and was just trying to spice up his life a little with Cherif's beautiful body, so I sort of understood what Cherif might be feeling. I told him that the woman didn't look like the kind to abuse kids and that she couldn't abuse me anyway because I could always jump off the massage table any time I wanted to, grab my clothes, and hightail it out of her parents' apartment. I also told him that she said she needed a letter from Daddy because of my age, so that made him feel better. After I went back to class I wondered what I would have done if Cherif had told me he didn't want me to have the massage. It was Mrs. Herrman's class and she was talking about how salmon reproduce which was kind of interesting, like with the frogs lesson, except that she makes even interesting things boring. So I thought that if Cherif had told me I couldn't have the massage – of course he couldn't tell me I couldn't, but he could tell me if I did he'd be all mad and everything – that probably would have been the beginning of the end of Cherif and me. I think the worst thing you can do in a relationship is to try to control the other person. Of course everybody is trying to get things from the other, but if the other feels pressure to be this or that or do this or that, it ain't no good... as Shakespeare used to say.

Earlier I said the blind woman saw with her ears. She sees with her hands too. The massage was kind of everything I had expected and more – something which doesn't happen too often in life. At least when the "more" is a positive more…. And by the way the blind woman has a name: Linda. I thought it was kind of ironic: Laura…Linda. Five letters each and each beginning with L and ending in a. Maybe ironic is not the right word. How about "coincidental" or "telltale"? Or maybe just "amusing" or "cute"? Whatever.

I had to ask her what her name was. When I did I already had all my clothes off (except my underpants – I refuse to wear a string…) and I was sitting on the massage table in her parents' spare bedroom looking at a bunch of old pictures on the wall. Linda's parents are about eight-five and move around about as fast as cars with no wheels, but they were real nice to me and said they had seen me in the neighborhood and at the supermarket across the street. I actually got there before Linda and her dog did, so I had a few minutes to talk to them and look at all the old stuff in their apartment. I guess when you live in the same place for fifty years and you don't change furniture and pictures on the wall and stuff, eventually everything starts looking real old-fashioned. I mean usually when you go to an old old person's house everything not only looks like it was made about a hundred years ago, but smells like it too. Then after a few minutes you get used to the smell and then it's just the "looking old" that gets you. If you're Linda, once you get past the smell, stuff probably just "feels" old.

Anyway, her parents were very nice and gave me a glass of fruit juice and we talked for ten minutes until Linda showed up. They asked me if I liked living in Switzerland and I gave my standard dumb – but true – answer: "It took a while to get used to things, but now I love it." Which would probably be the same thing for all the old junk in Linda's parents' apartment if I stayed in there for a few years….

So I was sitting on the massage table in my underpants kind of running my hands over my arms to keep warm while Linda was washing her hands and getting her massage oil and towel ready. The room wasn't really cold, but when you first take your clothes off it always feels a little chilly, even in a doctor's office or under the covers. It was actually really fun stripping down with her standing there in the same room because I'd say it was the first time I'd taken my clothes off with another person or people around and he or she or they didn't try to sneak a look at me or anything. You know, like in gym class girls are always trying to check each other out and hide their own bodies unless they look like Brigitte Bardot or Pamela Anderson about a hundred years ago, in which case they're trying to make everybody else jealous by showing off their big boobs and whatnot…. Or even when I have taken things off in front of Marcel Monnet or Cherif, their eyes were so focused on my skin they might as well have been crawling on my skin, if you know what I mean. But, since Linda couldn't see, it was like taking my clothes off in the dark with nobody around....

Anyway, finally Linda's all ready to get to work and she feels her way over to the table and feels that I'm still sitting there, so she tells me to lie down on my stomach with my head in a little hole at the end of the massage table. Then she runs her hands all over me real quickly which felt like mice were running across a field and I was the field. I guess she was trying to see how big I was and get an overview of what she was going to be massaging. She asked me how tall I was and I said one meter and sixty-nine centimeters and I added that I weighed about fifty-five kilograms. She didn't say anything. Then she put some more oil on her hands and immediately went to work on the back of my legs. I closed my eyes and about a million thoughts started running through my head without me inviting any of them to be there.... Had she been blind all her life? When was the last time she massaged someone? Did she prefer massaging men or women? Had she ever made love with a man or a woman? If so, was it someone she had encountered right here in this room on this massage table? Assuming she had been blind all her life, what was her idea of "beauty"? Whatever it was, had it been formed by touch only, or were smell and sound a part of it? Would music be her main source of "beauty" (like sometimes I think classical is for Daddy)? What did I smell like to her? Was being blind part of the reason she had such soft hands? Why did her hands feel like they each had extra fingers? When was she going to ask me for the letter from my father that was in the pocket of my pants hanging on the back of the chair next to the window? Did she really need a letter to massage a minor? Had she massaged a minor before and engaged in a little hanky-panky? …

To try to change the subject in my head, I decided to talk. "That sure feels good," I said. "I love having the back of my legs massaged."

"Have you had many massages in your life?" she said.

"Maybe three or four."

This was half true. Other than my mother massaging my head and arms when I was maybe seven years old and had a fever, Cherif had given me exactly two massages, but each time I could tell that all he was thinking about was getting the massage over with as quickly as possible so we could make love.

"How long have you given – did you give – massages?" I asked.

"Oh, for about eight years."

"That's how old I was when my mother died."

I thought my telling her that my mother had died when I was young would kind of give us something in common, like I had a disability too and so we shared something. Then I thought what if she didn't consider being blind a disability? What if it was just what she was used to and it was stupid and condescending of me to think she saw herself as "disabled"?

We were both silent for a while. Suddenly she said, "Excuse me, but I don't think you've told me your name, have you?"

"Laura."

"That's a nice name."

She didn't say anything about the similarity.

"And you said you were sixteen?"

"Yes."

She didn't say anything about the letter from my father. But it definitely didn't matter because I could tell already that if she did try to touch any of my pieces of deluxe jewelry, it would be okay with me and it surely wouldn't be without my consent and I surely wouldn't be one to take a blind woman to court....

"I went to massage school when I was eighteen. It took three years to get my diploma. Then I gave massages for... like I said... about eight years. Then I stopped when I was twenty-nine to travel with my mother," Linda said.

How does a blind person travel? What do they "see"? What do most travelers "see"? Maybe a blind traveler "sees" as much or more than a regular two-eyed traveler. Maybe Linda "saw" more because she didn't go around looking at a bunch of tourist junk. Maybe I'm full of a bunch of "merde"?

"Where did you go?" I asked.

"We went to India and Thailand and Hong Kong. My mother wanted to see the Orient. We traveled for about six months?"

"Did your father go, too? By the way, your parents are very nice."

"No, he was working. It was just my mother and me. We stayed the longest in India. Three months."

Should I ask her what she remembers most?

"What do you remember most?"

"About India or everything?"

"Everything?"

"Oh India. India for sure. There were people everywhere. Noise everywhere. The smell of spices everywhere."

She started rubbing the back of my thighs. She felt around for my underpants and pushed them up so she could also rub the bottom part of my buns.

"When we came back to Lausanne," she said, "I stopped giving massages. I really wanted to travel some more. But we didn't have the money to do it. I started reading a lot... braille of course... about other places in the world."

"So now, how often do you give a massage?"

"Oh, not very often. Maybe once a month. To friends."

"Well, thanks for doing me."

She didn't say anything.

Had she met a man – or a woman – on the job and had she fallen in love and had her heart broken and that's why her mother had taken her on that trip and that's why she didn't want to massage anymore? Because she was afraid it would happen again?

She put oil on my thighs. Then she started on my lower back. She pushed the underpants halfway down my buns. She put oil on my back. When she did the upper part of my back she came around to the front of the table so my head was where her legs were. After she finished the back she did each arm and all the fingers and the middle of each hand. Then she came back to the front and did the back of my head and neck.

When she finished my head and neck she told me to turn over. She went to the other end of the table and put oil on her hands and first did my feet and toes. Then my ankles, calves, knees and thighs. She spent the most time on my feet and thighs. She asked me what I wanted to do in life.

"I have a few more years of school to do, I guess. I don't know what I want to do after that. The truth is I haven't thought about it very much."

"You're still young. You have time."

This time, next time, last time, every time, never, sometimes, often, usually, hardly ever, once in a while, the first time, the second time, the last time… yeah, she's right. Time is all I have.

She rubbed my midriff very lightly and then my ribs. She put more oil on her hands before she lightly massaged the under part of my breasts. Then she did my face very gently and finished with the area around my temples.

I got dressed and asked her how much I owed her. Daddy had given me five twenty-franc bills. She refused to take any money. I said goodbye and gave sixty francs to her mother on the way out. At first she wouldn't take anything either, but I said my father would be very unhappy if I brought all the money back to him. She finally took it after I insisted she buy something for Linda. I almost suggested a bottle of perfume. I asked her if Linda had been blind all her life. She said yes, that's how she was born.

The Beatrice woman came over to dinner last night. Like Daddy said, she was very nice and seemed extremely intelligent. By that I mean we could talk about anything. It seems the smarter people are, the more open they are to discussion about pretty much any topic under the sun. With dumb people you can't really talk about anything except certain subjects like what they believe in and what the weather is like in Hawaii. Some smart people can be dumb too when they think they're the only ones who are smart and they don't let anybody else say anything without trying to make them feel dumb. Smart smart people let dumb people say all their dumb stuff and even let them feel good about saying it. Dumb smart people keep interrupting them all the time or making "te-te" sounds to try make the other person look dumb. Real smart smart people think that people really never change very much and so they pretty much let everybody be what they are and believe all the junk they believe because there's no way in a million years that they're all of the sudden going to have a different brain that sees the world suddenly differently....

Anyway, this Beatrice woman made me feel comfortable saying anything I wanted to say and I could tell Daddy liked her because he was talking about things that he doesn't talk about with everybody, like dying and killing yourself and how maybe one day democracy will be replaced by some "enlightened monarchs" – or something like that. Most people think democracy is as sacred as clean underwear, but Daddy thinks it has lots of disadvantages like voting for dumb presidents and congressmen and women and voting to stop building minarets but continuing to build other churches, etc. etc.... What I mean is that it's nice to have somebody come to dinner who isn't like a Jehovah's Witness or an ecologist or communist or whatever who sees the world in all black and white and everything is either good or bad or the work of God or the Devil. One time this psychiatrist guy came to dinner with his wife and that was almost worse than having a Jehovah's Witness because you could tell that everything you said was getting psychoanalyzed and you really felt like just another patient lying on the guy's flucking couch (I haven't used that word for a while) ....

One thing that was interesting about Beatrice was that even though she was about sixty-five, she had this long grey hair that she let hang down like she was doing a hairspray commercial or something. I mean most older women either dye their hair or cut it short so there's not so much grey to look at... but she wanted you to see it like she was proud of it, just like some of the girls at school who wear the low low-cut blouses so everybody can see what they've got. I wondered if I ever get to sixty-five if I'll let my grey hair grow long and comb it all fluffy and everything like I'm proud of it, or if I'll cut it off or make it black or dark brown or red to make me look younger from the back but not much younger from the front. The age of sixty-five used to look like about nine million light years away, but for some reason these days it sometimes looks like it's just around the corner. I'm not sure if that's a bad sign or a good sign....

Anyway, I even told Daddy and Beatrice about my massage. I mean about how I felt during my massage. I mean about it being maybe the sexiest moment of my life. I explained how all of the sudden I had this feeling that Linda's hands had more eyes in them than any regular eyes, and that her hands on my body was like the first time anybody had really "seen" my body and that for some reason I said to myself that this was a sexier moment than the moments I've had with my boyfriend that are supposed to be all sexy and everything, but when all is said and done maybe shouldn't be called sexy, but should be called something like blind love. I mean the whole thing wasn't easy to explain, but Daddy and Beatrice listened to me and let me fumble around with my thoughts and stuff. When I said that when Cherif and I do stuff we're both kind of "blind" and when Linda was doing stuff she seemed like she could really "see", both Daddy and Beatrice acted like I was making some kind of sense. At the end we started talking about the difference between sexual and sensual and Beatrice said that in our world they're definitely not synonyms, but in a better world maybe they would be. Daddy didn't say much. I think he was enjoying hearing the girls and he was enjoying the wine. He even gave me a couple of sips. The only thing he did say was that the older he got the more the sexual side of life reminded him of eating or going to the toilet. He didn't say anything about the sensual side.

I have to tell you about another film we saw in school today. When I say I have to tell "you", of course I mean I have to tell myself which is kind of a lonely feeling, but maybe someday somebody will read my junk and feel like we're actually talking together....

We had a big English test on Thursday about the present perfect tense and we had to memorize all the irregular verbs… go-went-gone, see-saw-seen, teach-taught-taught, come-came-come (that one is really dumb), cut-cut-cut, put-put-put, hit-hit-hit, sit-sat-sat (makes a lot of sense, doesn't it?) etc. etc.… Anyway for me it wasn't too hard because I know them pretty much without thinking, but the other kids had to learn about eighty of them. So today, Friday, we had two periods in a row of English and the teacher said we could choose any film we wanted again (remember the ghetto one with everybody shooting each other and saying fluck all the time). Well, this boy named Bryan brought a film called "Bad Boys II" with Will Smith. Believe it or not, I had never seen a Will Smith film or "Bad Boys I" or, for that matter, even a real big-time "action" film. Of course I've seen Will Smith's picture plastered all over the place and I've seen snippets (what a great word…somebody should put it in the Language Hall of Fame…) of action films on TV and in previews at the cinema, but I had never actually sat down and watched one…. Well, ladies and gentlemen of the jury, what I saw was some of the absolute worst shit I have ever seen in my life – and I should not use the word shit alone, but should put some adjectives like "trashy" "junky" "worthless" "moronic" "disrespectful" "vacuous" and "insane" in front of it. What I'm trying to say is: Where and what has the world come to? How has the world come to this point? What kind of world are we living in?… where people can watch two hours and twenty minutes of death, destruction and violence, where bodies are blown all over the screen, dead bodies are falling out of trucks onto freeways and are getting run over by cars and trucks, cars and trucks are flying through cities at ninety miles-an-hour and smashing cars and trucks and people that are exploding and starting enormous fires, people are shooting guns out of both hands or high-powered machine-guns at each other like it is a sport and the dead disappear from the screen in a nanosecond never to be heard from again, and all this in what is supposed to be a reasonably civilized part of the planet... the city of Miami.... And the kids around me watched it like they were eating cornflakes, like it was the most normal thing in the world. Hey, maybe I'm the one who's not normal... Or maybe it's rather certain I'm the one who's not normal, because after the film when I tried to say a thing or two to a couple of friends about how films like this might be affecting the minds of people (people our age and younger in particular, but I didn't say as much) by making death and violence as banal as breakfast, they all just kind of laughed and said it was a cool film and that Will Smith was cool and that's it's just a movie. But I can't help but think the world is headed down the toilet. Maybe it's always been headed down the toilet.... I mean look at what Cortez did to the Aztecs – and when we "learned" about that in school it was "normal" and Cortez even looked like the good guy...

I'd better go to bed. Cherif and I are going skiing tomorrow. He doesn't have a rugby game and the ski season is almost over.

22)

I decided to make a chapter again. I decided I like chapters. After thinking about that film, I decided I needed a chapter, maybe like an old woman with no husband or money needs to go into a church to get a breath of fresh stale air. I mean she needs to smell that old smell that she's smelled for years that gives her a lousy hope that hope exists. Chapters give me hope that maybe there's a separation between "Bad Boys II" and other parts of the planet earth. I just don't see how people can spend all that time and energy and money to crash all those cars and make all that noise with guns and start all those fires and smash all those things to smithereens. Of course the only real reason they do it is to make money, so that tells you everything right there. When we were on the train going up to the mountains to ski, I told Cherif about it (actually he kind of has a smile like Will Smith) and he told me that he has watched a whole bunch of action films and they haven't made him crazy or violent or want to shoot somebody. I told him that it's obviously different for people who live in the ghetto because there they really do shoot each other. I read a story in the newspaper yesterday about a big NBA basketball star named Danny Granger who was raised in the ghetto in New Orleans and he said he got shot in the leg when he was twelve and one of his friends got shot about twenty times... and never died! I mean some people are actually SHOOTING those guns. Daddy says if he were president the first thing he would do is ban all guns and that's why he has no chance to be president (of course he has less than zero chance anyway). Getting rid of guns in America would probably be harder than starting my education revolution. In America people think it's a God-given right to carry a gun. It sure isn't a Jesus-given right. Can you imagine Jesus carrying a gun? I'll bet if Jesus came back to earth, he'd ban guns too. Yet half the creamy Christians in America act like if they can't have a gun next to their bed or on the rack in their pick-up truck the Devil is running the country. Daddy says that everybody's God corresponds to what they want, not what God wants. Of course he doesn't believe in any kind of God, but he says that if you look at the world, all the Gods that were invented correspond to the people that invented them. He also says that what people think is good and evil always suits their lifestyle and tradition. He says Buddhism had the Far East, Islam had the Middle East, and American Christianity had the Far West... or something like that. Anyway, I can't wait to go to Marrakesh to see what that's like. We leave a week from yesterday.

Back to school.... There was a special play kind of thing all the older students had to go to this morning instead of having French class. It was some actors doing a sketch on what you should do if you (a girl) want a guy to wear a condom when you make love (or whatever you want to call it) and he doesn't want to because he says he couldn't possibly have AIDS because he's been a good boy all his life and condoms take away part of the pleasure and blah, blah, blah…. First I wondered if they have such things for sixteen-year-olds in America. Then I thought this is actually a pretty good thing because after the actors did a scene, the lady who was running the show came out and asked us if we would have said or done something differently than the actors – like when the girl finally gives in to the guy and says she won't make him wear the condom. I finally got up the nerve to raise my hand and I went up and played the girl and I told the guy that I didn't care if he was Will Smith, if he didn't put that rubber on he wasn't "getting inside the treasure chest" … which at least made everybody laugh and turn and look at Cherif who was sitting with his class a couple rows behind mine. But what I thought was really interesting was that after the show we went back to class for a few minutes and the French teacher asked us a few questions about how we liked the thing. Then he said that he thought they should also have talked about how kids react when they find out that their boyfriend or girlfriend has done it with somebody else behind their back. He subtly asked the class how we would react. Most kids had violent reactions like "I'd slap her in the face" or "I'd beat up both her and the guy" or "I'd get my brother to beat him up" … Anyway, of course

I thought about "Bad Boys II", but I also thought about how most people are really really really dumb (and I'm thinking about all the TV and movies I've seen and books I've read) to not just say, "Hey, I guess that means you don't love me quite as much as I thought you did, and hey, you can go ahead and screw whoever you want to, but I don't want to be your girlfriend (or boyfriend) anymore, and so...see you!!!" But instead what happens is that people take it all personally and feel all hurt and upset and think the world is coming to an end. What they should do is say, "Hey, it's your loss, not mine. Now I just know you're not my person." I know it's all easier said than done, but I think schools should teach kids not to be such morons when it comes to the great game of Major League Love. At least I hope that if and when Cherif and I have a "problem", I'll be able to look at it with a semblance of a brain and not get all hysterical and crap. Now that Cherif and I are past the all "gah-gah goo-goo eyes" stage I can sort of tell that the odds are about one in six hundred and twenty-four million that we'll stay together for life.... Anyway, the French teacher said he would suggest a show on the subject of breaking up which I thought was a really good idea.

Speaking of Major League Love, Snickers and Caramel have got me wondering what's going on in that cage. After I saw Snickers look like he (she?) was trying to mount Caramel (she? he?) and I got to thinking that there might be an egg that was going to get laid pretty soon, I put a nest in the corner of the cage and some string-like junk around so they could play at redecorating the nest to their liking.... Anyway, everybody tells me that normally it's only the female that hangs out in the nest all the time and that the male keeps bouncing around from branch to branch trying to look all macho and stuff and guarding the roost. Well, in our case Snickers and Caramel hang out together in the nest. In fact they sleep there every night! I'm wondering if they might be lesbians or something because they sure look all lovey-dovey in there... or maybe Snickers really is a male, but he just likes sleeping with Caramel every night. And then, given that there's only one bed in the inn, where else is he (she?) supposed to sleep? On a branch all his (her) life? For all I know, they're both males and when Snickers was trying to mount Caramel he was doing the male homosexual thing. I guess we'll just wait to see if an egg ever shows up. Maybe I should ask Mrs. Herrman. Now that I think about it, don't chickens on chicken farms lay eggs without a man in the house??? And aren't the eggs we buy in the store the kind that never get fertilized??? I'll check with Mrs. Herrman after we get back from Marrakesh....

23)

Dear Marrakesh,

I'm writing to you to thank you for letting Daddy and me stay with you for four days this past week. It was really fun and interesting and I thought you might like to know about some of the high points of our trip. I know you're not a person and normally people write letters to people, but to me you were kind of like discovering an old grandmother I didn't know I had. So I figured I'd write to you anyway and tell you about some of the things you allowed me to experience.

First of all, after we got our luggage, changed some money, and walked out of the airport, Daddy asked a taxi driver if he knew of any good riads to stay in because Daddy said it would be more fun to stay in the old medina than in New Marrakesh where everything is modern and the rich people and foreigners live. The driver was named Youssef and even though he kind of had a face that could have played the part of a serial killer in some dumb Hollywood film like "Bad Boys XIII" or something, he was really nice and helpful and friendly. It was also good that he spoke decent English and French. Actually "spoke" is the wrong word – he sort of "shouted" all the time as if Daddy and I were both three-quarters deaf. Not only did he shout, but most words – especially long ones – came out accompanied by cute sparkling saliva balls that popped out of all corners of his mouth. My daddy sometimes spits too when he talks, but Youssef made him look like an amateur. I think it was all just his enthusiasm more than anything else. He loved his city and he wanted us to love it too. We ended up using him as our driver all four days whenever we wanted to go somewhere.

Before I go any further I should say that Youssef wasn't a real "taxi" taxi driver because he didn't have a sign on top or on the side of his car that said "taxi". I think he really was just a guy who had a car who was doing anything he could to make a living. And what a car! It was an old beat-up Fiat Uno that he treated like a brand-new Mercedes, except that it looked like he hadn't cleaned it out or washed its face since he adopted it five years ago! I always sat in the back seat and would always be leaning forward to hear what he and Daddy were saying. I noticed that the red light was always on to say that he was almost out of gas. On the third day I decided to ask Youssef about it. He said, "Don't worry, I know my car," and he caressed the dashboard with his long greasy fingers like it was a woman's back. He was pretty tall compared to most people we saw in the streets and he must have weighed just a little more than me and I don't even weigh sixty kilos! Anyway, he and his car might be the thing I'll remember most about Marrakesh when I'm old and grey and looking back on life like the woman in the film "Titanic".

So anyway, Youssef took us to a riad that he said he used to work in (I can't imagine how many different jobs he's probably had in his life!) and which was right around the corner from where he lived. He said he was fifth generation Marrakeshian, but that his parents and most of his aunts and uncles were dead, so the house was all his. He was maybe forty years old at the most. He parked his car out on a street that was so full of people and donkey-pulled carts and bicycles and motor-scooters that you could hardly walk down it, much less drive a car down it. In fact Youssef was one of the only people who ever did! From where he parked the car, we walked down a couple of narrow alleys to a place that didn't even have a sign on the door. Of course Daddy and I both thought this was a little strange and that maybe something fishy was going on, but Youssef rang the doorbell and this real nice cute woman answered and said that they had a room, and in we strolled into a genuine "riad" riad with a courtyard with a bunch of plants and open rooms around it. (The manager told us later that there are now more than a thousand riads inside the medina!) Anyway, thanks for letting us stay in one of your riads. They're a great place to sleep and to get a feel for what your heart is really like.

After we got settled into our room (which you can't lock by the way, but there is a safe to put your valuables in) we went up onto the terrace on the roof and had a glass of very sweet mint tea with the manager. From the terrace we could see all of you including all your minarets, satellite dishes, and TV antennas. Off in the distance the Atlas Mountains kind of looked like the Swiss Alps, except hotter. Daddy and I went up there every evening and he always had a glass of white wine and I'd have a Coca-Cola Light and by the end of our stay I'd say it was kind of our sacred place to be. I'll never forget your orange light when the sun was going down or when the loudspeakers in your minarets started telling everybody it was time to pray and thank Allah for all the goodies in the world. I felt like I was on another planet, which in a sense I was.

So that first day, after we finished our tea with the manager (and he had told us a lot about his life: he was a thirty-year-old Romanian who had left the country during Ceausescu's reign of terror, had joined the French Foreign Legion, and had recently married a Moroccan woman which he could only do after converting to Islam) Daddy and I went for a walk. And let me tell you, taking a walk in your streets is like taking a walk in no other place I've ever been to! First the streets themselves – alleys mostly – are so narrow that sometimes two fat people would have to turn bellybutton to bellybutton to get by each other. Also, there are human beings of all ages all over the place and these loud motor-scooters are whizzing by so fast all the time that I always thought they were some kind of mini-ambulances taking people to emergency rooms in hospitals, but there was never anybody on the back. After we walked about five minutes we were already in the middle of the huge covered market where you have to bargain to buy anything, and, unless you walk really fast – which is almost impossible because of all the people – you get accosted about every five feet by somebody standing in front of a shop ("stall" is a better word) who is totally ready to sell you the-greatest-piece-of-something-you-absolutely-don't-need-in-the-history-of-the-universe! They can be pushy and obnoxious sometimes, but I guess they're just trying to make a living. After that first time through though, Daddy and I pretty much tried to avoid that area. We were able to find our little souvenir stuff on the side streets outside the famous Marrakesh Mall (that's what Daddy called the main market).

After we got through there we went to the big square (I can't remember the names of any of the places, but I'm sure you know where I mean) where there are about nine million food stands with somebody standing in front of each one telling you their food is the best in town. It reminded me of North Beach in San Francisco where there are all these strip clubs with a guy out front informing you that the most beautiful women in creation are waiting inside "just for you" (telling all the men that is...when they saw me they shut up). Daddy took me there once in the daytime and even then it was wild. So we ate a couscous dinner that probably cost less than a pack of french fries at McDonald's in Switzerland. That's what Daddy said, anyway. Then as it was starting to get dark, we walked around the square where there were actual live cobras dancing while some guy was playing a flute. (San Francisco: naked women dancing; Marrakesh: naked cobras dancing.) We watched from a distance as neither of us are great lovers of crawling animals, with or without legs. A couple of times we saw some tourists get up close to the snakes and the next thing they knew some guy had come up behind them and put another snake on their necks!!! The whole idea was to try to sell something, but I couldn't quite see how scaring the royal pucky out of somebody would get them to buy anything…. But your people seem to be trying to scrounge out a living any way they can. I guess it's that way all over the world, but you just don't notice quite so much in Europe and America.

On the last day of the trip, Youssef was taking Daddy and me to this beautiful blue-painted garden where Yves Saint-Laurent used to hang out (evidently he helped make Marrakesh famous for dumb tourists like us) and Daddy asked him what percentage of the local native people in the city believed that Allah was the God of the universe, that Mohammed was His prophet, and that the Koran was the word of God. Youssef said about 100% which – Daddy explained to me later – means that your people really are kind of on their own planet in that they really can hardly imagine that there is a "rest of the world" out there where there are all kinds of other religions with all kinds of other gods and sacred books and all that. Daddy said it reminded him of some of the people in his own family who believed their Protestant sect was the absolute total one-and-only truth about the world and they were so caught up in their little cocoon that they absolutely couldn't envision anything else. Daddy said that he could understand this a few thousand or even a few hundred years ago when people never traveled more than a few miles from their homes and had no idea what was going on in Samoa or Somalia or South Dakota (or even had a clue that these places existed…) and who thought the world was flat and didn't move and all that kind of thing. But today??? With internet and TV and books and libraries and movies and all the crap we have??? How can people NOT see that they are NOT alone on the planet and that they basically only believe what they believe because THAT'S WHAT THEIR TRADITION BELIEVED? Anyway, Daddy and I were both fascinated by how the Muslim culture was so powerful and so different from our stuff in the big rich Christianity-soaked Western world. Actually, when you think about it, it's really different on the surface, but maybe deep down inside people are pretty much the same everywhere. They just come from different parts of the world. On the plane ride back home Daddy said that all Middle-Americans (I'm only capitalizing "middle" for symmetry) should go to Middle-Marrakesh and all Middle-Marrakeshians should go to Middle-America for a great big exchange program and that maybe then the world might have a chance at world peace and harmony and brotherhood and understanding and all that kind of Santa Claus good cheer stuff. Daddy's always talking about how people should try to see outside their little boxes, but he knows it's a pretty hard thing for the human head to do, and, if you want to know the truth, sometimes I think that he thinks that it's more or less impossible....

Oh well... I just want to say thanks for everything. Thanks for the sounds of the motorbikes and the Arab people talking and the minaret callers calling. Thanks for the smells of the marketplace and the food stands and the exotic perfumes. Thanks for the colors of the clothes and the pottery and the people's skin and eyes. Thanks for the delicious fresh-squeezed orange juice in the main square that cost about ten cents. And finally, thanks for the blue sky and the hospitality that you showed Daddy and me, two straggly tourists from another corner of the planet that we English speakers call "the earth".

Sincerely,
your friend
Laura Winger

Of course I didn't send the letter. But I showed it to Daddy. He liked it. I also showed it to Cherif. He didn't seem to appreciate it as much as Daddy because he hadn't been there with us. It's never the same if you haven't been there. Actually Daddy said I should send it just for fun. He said I should send it to...

Marrakesh

Morocco

Africa

World

Universe

… just like kids do when they send a letter to God or Santa Claus, and see what happens. Maybe I will. Daddy said sending it would kind of be like what writers do when they write books. They really have no idea who they're writing to or who will end up reading their stuff. He said writing was like throwing darts at the Milky Way. The whole thing kind of made me feel all cold and lonely for a while. I tried to explain this to Cherif too, but when I saw that he didn't really get what I was talking about, it just made me feel colder and lonelier. So first I put on a sweater and then I took it off and we made love. Both helped a little.

Since we came back from Marrakesh I have started to have a different feeling about Snickers and Caramel. I know it might sound stupid and that nobody in the universe gives a flying fluck about my feelings about my birds, but I thought it was interesting. First, when we walked in the door to the apartment – after being away for four days – I immediately went to their cage to see if they would have any reaction toward me. It's not like I expected them to jump up and down and start spinning in circles like dogs do when you come home, but, you know, I just wanted to see if they'd do a couple of nice chirps or wing flaps to show Daddy and me that they were glad to see us. Well, the truth is, I think they were kind of scared because all they did was stay huddled together in their nest and look around left and right every few seconds like a light tower checking to see if any ships were about to crash or something. I mean, I think all they really cared about was being together in that cage and having nobody mess with them. Of course they probably wanted to be sure somebody was filling up their birdseed trough and water bottle, but I don't think it mattered if it was me or the man on the moon. After a few minutes they started chirping and fluttering around again, but that was after I had gone into my room to unpack and Daddy was in the kitchen making something to eat.

The second thing is, I'm starting to wonder if Snickers and Caramel aren't sort of like the people who have lived in the same place all their lives and are totally satisfied with their situation because it's totally what they're used to and they don't know anything else. I mean if Snickers and Caramel had been born in the wild and had flown around freely for a few months or years and THEN somebody had caught them and stuck them in a little cage for the rest of their lives, that would be one thing. But they were BORN in a cage and have ALWAYS LIVED in a cage! So they absolutely don't know anything else. The longer I watch them flutter around, the more I'm convinced that they're NOT UNHAPPY, just like most of the poor people I saw in Marrakesh didn't seem to be unhappy. The more I think about it, the more I think I can compare my birds to not only the people in Marrakesh, but also the people in New York City or Paris or Pleasant Hill or Buenos Aires or on the moon for that matter. I mean when you really think about it, ALL EXISTENCE comes from a PERSPECTIVE. Who on earth is able to judge another creature's perspective? And who is to say how another creature REALLY feels about his or her or its situation? If you're from the Bronx in New York and listen to hip-hop all day and walk around with baggy pants falling off your butt and you're wearing sunglasses and a T-shirt that's eight times too big for you and you've got no father, but you've got a dooo-raggg on your head and a couple joints and packs of rubbers in your pocket etc. etc.… your perspective is going to be a little tiny bit different than that of the Mormon missionary that Daddy and I saw yesterday in Lausanne who's walking around in a black suit and tie and white shirt and is carrying a Book of Mormon in his hand that's telling him about angels and Holy Ghosts and his place in heaven after he lives a life of never drinking coffee, tea, beer, wine, or whisky and never cheating on his wife of fifty-nine years, the last fifty of which see them never making love because they don't want any more kids, and your hair is nicely cut and parted on the side and you have maybe a mint and a piece of chewing gum in your pocket. Et cetera. Et cetera. And on and on and on until it never stops.…

So what I'm trying to say is that all my anthropo-morphic (remember that word from page two?) judgements about Snickers and Caramel might be as off the wall as the ghetto kid judging the Mormon missionary or the Mormon missionary judging the ghetto kid or the Moroccan judging the American or the French judging the Chinese or the judge judging the criminal or the moon judging the sun or a carrot judging a pickle or a worm judging a fish or a fish judging a worm or a six-year-old judging a grandmother or a criminal judging a judge or the wind judging the rain or a dog judging a cat...

I can't help thinking about all this stuff. Sometimes I wish I could just put on an iPod and listen to the Black-Eyed Peas say "Tonight's gunna be a good night" over and over about a hundred times and think everything is as simple as when Cherif and I first met and he walked me home from school and we flirted by ambling slowly and bumping arms every two seconds.... But something tells me... Snickers and Caramel tell me... Marrakesh tells me... Linda and Mrs. Herrman tell me... everything tells me... that it's not quite that simple.... Have I read too many books? Have I been around Daddy too much? If Mommy hadn't died would I be a cheerleader in Pleasant Hill? We'll never know, will we?

So good night birdies. Good night Cherif. Good night Daddy. Good night Mrs. Herrman. Good night Linda. Good night Marrakesh. It must be after midnight and school starts again tomorrow.

24)

After all that we need a new chapter. I say "we" facetiously. I had to look that one up. Facetiously, not we. My Fat Red American Heritage says it comes from…(I know you're holding your breath)…Old French facetieux, from facetie, a jest, from Latin facetia (should be a line over the "e"), from facetus (another line), elegant, fine, facetious. I had put an "i" instead of an "e". Actually I could have messed up "we" too by writing "oui" if I hadn't been paying attention.

School's been on for a week since Easter vacation. How much more can I take? And after this year I'm supposed to go to the "gymnase" which is another three years before I go to "l'universite" which is another four years. This morning a kid threw a handful of chalk at Mrs. Herrman while she was writing on the blackboard. When she turned around everybody looked all innocent and angelic, especially the kid – Miguel – who threw it. He had his arms crossed and this look in his eyes like he was looking at his dead grandmother or something. What's crazy is that Miguel is really not a bad kid, but he's always touching all the girls all the time and he's got all this energy and he can't sit still for more than three seconds, so every now and then he does something stupid like throw a handful of chalk at an innocent boring teacher like Mrs. Herrman. I almost wanted to tell her it was Miguel and explain that he's really not a bad kid, but that it's the system that is all flucked up by making kids sit together all day in boring classrooms, etc... but that would have taken too long and Miguel probably would have got in trouble, so I sat there like everybody else looking as clean as a cherry tree in April. Mrs. Herrman was all red in the face and I felt sort of sorry for her and thought maybe she should change jobs but that it was probably too late and who would hire her anyway except maybe a supermarket which would mean a serious pay cut but at least she wouldn't get chalk thrown at her and wouldn't have to try to keep twenty-five wild animals occupied for forty-five minutes twenty-five times a week (that's how many periods teachers teach) and maybe she wouldn't get grey hair so fast (it was too late anyway) and have a nervous breakdown like lots of teachers.... Finally, after she had yelled her weak old-ladyish yell and tried to figure out who the culprit was, she said that if somebody didn't admit to throwing the chalk she was going to punish the whole class. Miguel then owed up to it which just goes to show you he's not a bad guy at all. He got two hours detention on Wednesday afternoon which I'm sure won't change his behavior one iota. (iota: 1. ninth letter of the Greek alphabet; 2. a very small amount. Often used in the phrase not one iota.) (Will somebody please tell me why ninth is spelled "ninth" instead of "nineth"? "Ninth" should be pronounced like "winth" or "sinth" which aren't even words, but should be if life was fair…) But my theory is that none of this would happen if we stopped putting kids in class six or seven hours a day and started using computer technology and all that…. But I'm repeating myself. You already know what I think.

But you don't know that I'm going to have another massage with Linda tomorrow morning. I saw her the day after we got back from Marrakesh. I was with Daddy, so he got to see her too. (Obviously she didn't get to see him.) She always looks kind of disheveled, but what do you expect given that she can't look at herself in the mirror. Anyway, when I introduced her to Daddy, they started talking and he was the one who suggested that she give me another massage and he insisted that he pay her. I guess his voice had some kind of an impact because she agreed to be paid fifty francs. Cherif has a rugby game in Bern so I won't be seeing him until maybe tomorrow night. After that first massage I kept thinking about the difference between a Linda massage and a Cherif massage, between her hands on my body and his hands on my body, between her mind attached to my body and his mind attached to my body. Then I thought about the reverse: Why would or wouldn't I want to put my hands on her body like I want to put them on Cherif's body? Why would or wouldn't my mind want to flow through my hands and melt into her body like it does into Cherif's body? What makes a lesbian a lesbian? What makes a straight a straight? What makes a chicken a chicken? A goat a goat?

Speaking of goats… I'm 99.999% sure I didn't tell you about the time Daddy and Cherif and I went to the Servion zoo which is in the hills behind Lausanne and only about fifteen minutes away. It was a couple of weeks ago on a sunny Sunday – it's spring now – so there were basically wall to wall cars in the parking lot, but not wall to wall people in the zoo because the zoo's pretty big inside. Anyway, we looked at the Siberian tigers and the bears and the lynxes and kangaroos and llamas and porcupines and foxes and wolves (white as snow by the way) and they all seemed to be having a reasonably good time and didn't seem too pissed off about living in a cage with a bunch of fools staring at them all the time, when suddenly we noticed that the biggest crowd of human animals was around the goat enclosure. Of course we were curious to know why because goats don't usually get nearly the press or play that tigers and bears do, so we walked over. There were a whole bunch of goats in the goat pen and we soon realized that three goats over by the water trough were getting all the attention. There was a mother goat and two babies and the babies had only been born a couple of hours before and to prove it there were still pieces of umbilical cord hanging from the babies' stomachs and the mother's rear end area was still all bloody and gooey-looking. What was amazing was that the babies were already walking! After two hours on earth… walking! I don't mean they were waltzing around like Fred Astaire and Ginger Rogers, but they were actually standing up and taking a few steps.

Personally I think they were looking for a restaurant, meaning a mommy tit, but that's beside the point. The point is that it takes humans a year to walk and these goats were walking after an hour. Not only were they walking but they looked like they knew what they were walking for… milk! Not like we human babies who – as soon as we can stand on two feet – start motoring around in any old crazy direction like some broken wind-up doll. Well, that got Daddy and me talking about how humans might be reasonably developed in some ways but not in others and all that crap. Then when we finally left the goats and went to the monkey cages and watched how unbelievably coordinated monkeys are, Daddy suggested that maybe monkeys evolved from humans and not vice versa. The whole trip to the zoo kind of blew my mind about where everything came from and what everything was doing and thinking and caring about and how miraculous and strange and unbelievable life is. I remember looking – I mean really looking looking – at the ostriches' eyes and wondering what they see and what was behind those eyes and that got me thinking about how eyes came about in the first place, and then how ears came about, and then noses, and then arms and legs and reproductive stuff and all of the sudden I thought my head was going to explode!!! I tried to get a feeling for how Cherif was seeing everything. I kind of got the impression that he was mostly thinking about getting back to the apartment so we could go to my room and make love, because he kept pinching me on the butt and putting his arm around my waist and then moving his fingers slowly up so he could touch the under part of my beautiful boobs (he's the one who tells me they're beautiful). When Daddy and I were talking about how amazing it was that all this stuff existed (us included), Cherif never said anything except once when he looked at the wolves and said they look just like dogs. I said they looked more like dogs than Chihuahuas look like dogs, but Cherif didn't say anything back. One of my favorite things about zoos is when people don't know what animal they're looking at and they go find the sign in front of the cage with a name on it, and they say "Oh, that's a so-and-so…" and they think they've understood something about the animal when all they've really done is tacked a dumb name to it which means absolutely nothing and tells them absolutely nothing about the life of the creature they're staring at. When you think about it, dictionaries – even Big Fat Red ones – kind of do the same thing all the time without anybody noticing it…words, words, words…that don't really cut under the surface, if you see what I mean.

Oh well…. Where was I before the goats sidetracked me? Oh yeah, the massage. I'm tired. I'll tell you tomorrow. I'll tell you what was going through my sixteen-year-old head while a fifty-something-year-old blind woman was massaging my sweet vanilla body.

Can you imagine? When blind people make love, the lights are always off.

25)

Do you remember Beatrice, Daddy's friend who lost everything? She came to dinner again last night. Cherif couldn't come over after his rugby game because he got back after nine and his mother said he couldn't go out. That was okay. I got to talk to Daddy and Beatrice. Daddy made his famous spaghetti. Normally people don't make spaghetti when they invite people to dinner because it's supposed to be some kind of an insult not to serve meat or fish, but Daddy says that just shows how dumb people are. Spaghetti can be the most delicious thing in the world, and I must admit Daddy makes a tomato sauce with lots of garlic and onions and cognac that is so good we both usually eat three plates. Anyway, Daddy didn't think Beatrice would be the kind of person to be insulted by being served spaghetti and I think he was right. She kept raving about how good it was and people don't usually rave if they think something is lousy. They usually just don't say anything.

What was interesting was that I kept thinking that for a person who had "lost" everything, Beatrice seemed like she "had" everything. I mean here she was, somebody with no more work to fill her time, no more husband hanging around, no more kids at home… and she never complained for one second about anything. Instead she talked about how she was enjoying the time she had to read and go to the cinema and see old friends that she hadn't seen for years. It was like the stupid expression about the glass half full or half empty... for her the glass was full which made it fun being around her. Other people would have been complaining about being all lonely and depressed and feeling like an old shoe because their husband had taken off with another woman etc., but not Beatrice. She acted like it was almost a good thing. It made me think that in everything there is the opposite, like in love there is hate, in friendship there is loneliness, the far is in the near, the up in the down, the empty in the full, the victory in the defeat, joy in suffering, life in death and death in life.... It might sound like a lot of crap, but as I was watching Beatrice eat her spaghetti and drink her wine with her grey hair combed like a homecoming queen and her smile making her wrinkles pinch together all the time, I thought. "Holy shit...it's people themselves that make life what it is or isn't... and it's people who create the opposites and decide which side of the fence to stand on...."

Anyway, Daddy enjoys her company and I do too.

But...but...but you...you...you probably could give a flying chicken feather about my yin and yang rambling talk. You want to know about what happened at MASSAGE NUMBER II. You, you being a card-carrying member of the human race, the dirtiest filthiest most lascivious-minded species on the face of the earth, you want to know what happened when Linda's hands combed my body for the second time. You want to know the "sexual side". Animals do sex in season and then forget about it. But not you – you think about it all year round. Hunting season never stops... And what I really love after sixteen years on earth, is that when animals do their sex stuff we humans never consider it a "moral" issue. No, no, no... we say it's "just part of nature". But when we humans do the sex stuff, it has nothing to do with nature and everything to do with morality.... Why can't everybody just admit that we're all roaming the jungle forever and ever....

But Linda... Back to Linda... She was PERFECTION. She totally outdid herself. She spent ten minutes on my feet, fifteen minutes and thirty-five seconds on my legs, fourteen minutes on my back, ten minutes and twelve seconds on my arms and fingers, five minutes on my stomach, five minutes on my head, and five minutes and fifty-nine seconds on my shoulders. (Of course I have absolutely no idea how long she spent on what, but I do know it was more than a sixty minute job!) It was more than an hour in heaven. More than an hour of having hands with eyes seeing and feeling – and I mean feeling – on my body. More than an hour of being as alive as a shooting star. More than an hour of having my eyes shut, but seeing Linda's hands seeing my body like no one has ever seen it before. And the second time is always better than the first. Well, not always. It depends on what... But what you want to know is what went on in my inner jungle.... That's what you want to know.... So I'll tell you. But in a whisper, in a soft soft whisper: It's none of your gooey-dooey business, you filthy-minded perverts who read all the people pages just to know who's popping who, you who sneak looks at porno on the internet, who have wet dreams and look at naked people in magazines and who can't even sit in church without having lustful thoughts about some piece of existence or other and who wake up in the middle of the night with a dog bone between your legs (I know, I've slept with Cherif) or a little spoonful of moist honey at the top of the tree. I know you. And I love you like I love life itself.... So goodnight everybody. Sleep tight, as tight as a belt around a fat man's waist.

26)

The more I write the more fun it gets. I can say anything, anything I want. Usually – in regular life I mean – you can't say what you want to say because somebody will get pissed off and you're supposed to be nice to people and all that kind of stuff. But in a book…whammo!…you can say whatever you gooey-dooey want to say. And if people don't want to read it, they can just close the book and toss it in the nearest garbage can. So if they do read stuff that pisses them off, it's all their own fault. Sometimes I get the feeling I could go on and on and on forever… for as long as I live, I mean. When you think about it, all life is is a long long book. People are talking to themselves all the time. Most people just don't write it down. Some people write it down and it's boring as hell and nobody wants to read it. Some people write it down and it's interesting as hell, but nobody understands it so nobody wants to read it. Some people write it down and don't even want anybody to read it. Some people write it down and it might even be boring as hell, but everybody wants to read it. Whatever. But in the end, reading books is really just getting to be friends with somebody you probably will never meet. I mean maybe you can go get an autographed copy at some dumb literary festival book signing or something, but there will most likely be a line so you won't get to talk to the author for more than five seconds and he or she probably won't even look at your face because he or she is tired and just wants to get on to the next person and get the book signing over with as soon as possible so he or she can go back to his or her hotel room or go have dinner or something… But that's okay. You still have the book. Most authors probably aren't nearly as fun to talk to in person as they are in their books. In person they don't have time to think about what they say before they say it. In books they have all the time in the world…

Speaking of the world. I got some news today from Daddy. He told me he might have something wrong inside him. He started out by talking about how amazing and complex and complicated the human body is and how it's a miraculous miracle that it functions as well as it does…all that Daddy kind of talk…and then he tells me that he's had a little pain for a while in the middle of that mushy jungle and that he finally went to a doctor this morning and the doctor told him it might be serious but they'd have to do a bunch of tests and talk to experts and everything. I told him not to bullshit me, but he said he wasn't. He said they won't be sure for a couple of weeks. He said that what was sure was that one day he won't be around anymore and I will have to fend for myself. He didn't really say it like that, but I know that's what he meant. Of course we've already talked about it and I've already thought about it about nine million times. I've wondered if, when the day comes, Cherif will still be around to help hold me up. I kind of doubt it. How many first loves last? Maybe six? But other people will show up. Something will be there. I've wondered if Snickers and Caramel will be there. Or Beatrice. Or Linda. Or a dog. Or books. Or music. Daddy has been listening to a lot of Tchaikovsky and Beethoven lately. It used to be Mozart. Mozart died young. Tchaikovsky killed himself. Beethoven went deaf. I guess if I've learned one thing in sixteen years it's that the road is not always rosy. But at least there's a road.

At school today the English teacher went off so loud and hard at Jerome that he lost his voice. Like I've said, he – the teacher – is a really nice guy and just tries to help us and everything and doesn't make a big deal about grades because he knows the only thing that matters is that we learn something and maybe learn not to be jerks along the way. And for him to go off there has to be a bunch of things leading up to it, just like that volcano up in Iceland that has stopped all the air traffic in northern Europe all the way down to Switzerland. I mean it doesn't just decide to blow... it's been simmering for a long time and suddenly it can't simmer anymore and something has to give and POOMMM!!! – a huge cloud of smoke starts circling the hemisphere. (The English teacher's explosion just circled the top floor of the school.) So what led up to it was that Jerome is all worried now that the end of the year is coming that he won't have the grades to be able to do another year and eventually have a chance at the university and all that, so he desperately counts up his points every day and begs every teacher to find a way to up his dumb grade point average… So, anyway, the English teacher told him that he (or anybody else in the class) could read a book (a pretty funny comic book about human beings being sheep who will believe anything) and he would give him a reading and comprehension test and if he understood absolutely everything he would give him the "6" (the best grade) he swears he needs to save his sorry scholastic ass. Jerome read the book and the teacher gave him the "6". I heard their conversation after and the teacher said, "Okay, Jerome, I've helped you, now you help me and be a good kid and a good influence on the rest of the class until the end of the year." Jerome said he'd do it and there's only a month of school left….

Well, this afternoon the teacher said we could see a film because it was Friday, but that he was going to choose it and there would be no discussion. I guess this was because he'd watched the students watching enough idiot violence in "Bad Boys II" and "Inglorious Bastards" – or whatever it was called. So he puts in the DVD and gets everybody to finally sit down and shut up and the DVD is Walt Disney's "Mulan II" (which, by the way, I thought was a really good movie…). So all of the sudden in the back of the class Jerome starts bitching and whining about "Mulan II" being a film for babies and morons and all that. The teacher jumped up from his desk, ran to the back of the class, and cussed out Jerome so badly that spit was flying out of all corners of his mouth even more than I've ever seen it come out of Daddy's. At one point Jerome tried to talk back to him, then the teacher really let him have it. I think that's when he lost his voice. At one point I almost started laughing when he screamed, "CAN'T YOU STOP BEING AN ASSHOLE FOR JUST FIVE MINUTES?" At the end I had the impression that Jerome finally realized what a total imbecilic jerk he had been because he didn't say another word through the whole film. The funny thing (the good thing) was that nobody said a word (which I guess meant that the whole class got the message) and it seemed like the other kids really actually liked the film and when the bell rang everybody came up and shook the teacher's hand all politely and said "goodbye" and "have a good weekend". Even Jerome did, which he never does.

Anyway, when I got home from school there was a short note on the table from Daddy. He said that he had seen the doctor again (I think two weeks have gone by since the last time) and that he had decided to take a little weekend trip to Venice with Beatrice. He said he was sorry that he hadn't warned me, but that they had hopped on a train at noon. He left me fifty francs for groceries and told me he'd be back Sunday night. He knows that I don't mind when he's gone a couple of days given that Cherif and I can do what we want...lol...(not that we can't figure out a way to do what we want anyway....) The only thing was, for some reason after what happened at school with the English teacher and

Jerome, I didn't really feel like doing anything with Cherif tonight. I just felt like sitting home, watching a little TV, listening to some music, and maybe talking to Daddy. So I'll do everything except talk to Daddy…

In the note he didn't say what the doctor said. I guess he didn't have time. But the fact that he's going to Venice (he should be there about now, it's almost seven o'clock) and that he took Beatrice along with him kind of makes me think that the news isn't so hot and that he wanted to go to some beautiful place to distract himself. I didn't read "Death in Venice" for nothing….

Cherif just called. We both said we were kind of tired. I told him about what happened at school with Jerome and the English teacher. For whatever reason, I didn't tell him Daddy was out of town.

27)

I've decided this will be the last chapter and this will be the end of the book. My first book. Maybe my last book, but I kind of doubt it because sometimes I've started looking more forward to writing than making love with Cherif.

I haven't been able to write anything for a week. You can probably guess why… Daddy got to Venice on that Friday night. The next morning he sent me this email:

Dear Laura,
Sorry I didn't get a chance to talk to you or write you a more thorough note before leaving for Venice. But on my way home from school (remember I only teach one class on Friday mornings) I stopped at the train station and noticed there was a train to Venice in an hour. I quickly called Beatrice to see if she might like a change of scenery, bought the tickets, went home to grab a few clothes and a toothbrush, and rushed to Quai 9….

We had a nice lunch in the train. As you know Beatrice is someone who is easy to talk to. One thing we talked about – one of her favorite subjects – is how people think what's good for them is good for everybody else. It sounds simple, but when you get down and think about it, it might be one of the most profound problems with the human head. Beatrice called it "the greatest fallacy in human thinking". Left-wingers (no pun intended Laura Winger) do it, right-wingers do it, anarchists do it, terrorists do it, almost all religious types do it (maybe Buddhists are smarter than that), dieticians do it, film critics do it, psychiatrists do it, parents do it, kids do it, and on and on. When you think about it, there is absolutely no guarantee that what is good for me should be – or would be – good for someone else.... Anyway, the trip passed like ten minutes.

We got to Venice a little after seven and just started wandering until we found a cozy hotel on the Grand Canal. In case you're wondering, we got separate rooms, mostly because I couldn't see any reason to keep Beatrice awake with my snoring or farting. Hell, for all I know she might have kept me awake with hers! Anyway, things are fine and Venice is all it's cracked up to be as far as beauty goes. I can't believe I (we) hadn't come here before. I promise I'll bring you here before…

…Yeah, before I die. The doctor gave me some rather shitty news about me having some kind of pancreatic cancer that has already spread to different countries like Liverland and Great Kidney. He said "we" would start treatment next week and see if "we" could slow things down. He said operating was really out of the question as it was "too late". I actually laughed when he said "too late" thinking "too late for what?" – not too late to catch a train to Venice or have a good plate of spaghetti, or listen to Snickers and Caramel chirp. Of course it was too late to keep me around for another hundred years, but it's always been too late for that.... He didn't really give me a calendar with the number of earthly revolutions (no relation to French or American revolutions) I might have at my disposal but said things didn't look too promising... and all that. But hey, we both know that I've known for a long time that things never look too promising because every creature that walks on or flies around the planet doesn't do so for very long. I mean, even if it's eighty years... hell, that's just a puff of smoke in the cosmic imagination.... I've been lucky enough to go more than sixty. I'd be an ungrateful bastard if I complained. I've been luckier than 99.999% of the creatures that pop out of eggs or wombs or however else they come to be. I've been lucky enough to have you and your mother and a few friends and good food, drink, a warm house and all the rest. For me to complain would be an insult to myself and the universe....

Speaking of which – the universe, that is – if there is one thing I hope I have passed on to you, it is a wonderment that anything exists at all. Like Albert Camus said, "There's only one real philosophical question: Why is there something and not nothing?" Of course the "why" part will probably never be answered, which makes the wonderment all the greater. Of course, we are very good at coming up with all kinds of answers, but when the chips are down, I think we have to admit that nobody has a clue.... Once you have the wonderment, you're just happy to be around, to have eyes and ears and fingers and a nose to take in a few of the goodies of the world. Well, I've had that chance, and like the Indian chief at the end of "Little Big Man", I won't complain about what time I have to check out of Hotel Earth. And whatever happens, I know you'll be able to take care of yourself... and I'll get you here to Venice before the curtain goes down. It's really one of the places on earth mankind can be proud of.

I guess I better get ready for breakfast. I got up early, took a walk and watched the sun rise, came back to write to you, and told Beatrice I'd meet her downstairs at eight. We older folks like the morning.

See you tomorrow night,

Love, Dad

So that's it. It happened. Well sort of. Of course I cried all over the computer keyboard as I was reading it. But the damn machine still works... though it's taken me a week to touch it again....

You know, that's really the thing about life: everything finally happens, one way or another. You wait for something; it comes and passes. Then you wait for something else; it comes and passes. Then something else, then something else... Of course some things you want to happen never happen, but those are different kinds of things. This thing, I knew would come; and it came. Sometimes I think Daddy has been preparing me for it for years, maybe ever since that trip to Disneyland after Mommy died. And you know what? He told me pretty straight, hardly a word of bullshit in the whole letter. And you know what else? Since he came back from Venice, nothing's really changed.

199

Find out more about Jon Ferguson
and his works at his author website:
www.jonfergusonbooks.com,
where you can also sign up for updates.

Please contribute an honest online review;
it's the easiest and most supportive thing a reader can do
for an author and/or a small independent press.
editor@hugejam.com